Committed (Atlanta's Finest Series)

Sharon C. Cooper

Copyright © 2022 Sharon C. Cooper

All rights reserved. No part of this book may be used or reproduced in any manner without written permission except in the case of brief quotations embodied in critical articles and reviews. For permission, contact the author at www.sharoncooper.net

ISBN: 978-1-946172-32-7

This story is a work of fiction. Names, characters, and incidents are either products of the author's imagination or are used fictitiously. Any resemblance to actual events, locales, organizations, or persons, living or dead, is entirely coincidental.

Acknowledgments

Huge shout out to Circle of Sisters (CoS) book club! I didn't forget Priya's kids, and thanks for the idea!

And

Brenda S. - You make writing fun, and you are the most patient person in the world! Lol! You're awesome, and I so appreciate you!

Claire F. - Everyone should have a friend like you! I can't imagine my life without you!

Prologue

"I *saw Dennis Stratton kill Joyce Hayes.*"

A shiver went through Fred as those words flowed around in his head while he pulled into his driveway. He parked his Toyota Corolla on the side of his house under the carport next to his brother's sports car.

On the ride home, all he could think was—had he done the right thing?

Had he done the right thing in talking to the assistant district attorney and the DA office's investigator?

Sure, confessing cleared his conscience, and hopefully, he'd get a good night's sleep for the first time in two weeks. But he wasn't sure adding to his initial statement had been a good idea.

They had asked him why he hadn't been more forthcoming when the detectives on the case questioned him weeks ago. All he could tell them was that he'd been afraid of how it would look if they'd known that not only had he been in the office that night, but he saw and heard everything leading up to the murder.

I hope I did the right thing.

Questions bombarded his mind as he stared out into the darkness of his backyard.

What if I should've kept my mouth shut? What if the ADA somehow starts thinking that I'm the murderer? What if she tries to pin everything on me instead of the actual murderer—the CEO of Leverage Construction company?

His life would be ruined. Even if he was just a custodial worker, he had built up a pretty good life for himself. What if....

Someone knocked on the car window, and Fred jumped in his seat, hitting his knee on the bottom of the steering wheel. Pain shot through his leg. His heart leaped into his throat. Breathing hard, he jerked his head to the left and saw the person standing outside the driver's side window.

Christ.

He released the breath that had gotten stuck in his chest and dropped back against the cloth seat.

Omar.

His brother had scared the crap out of him. Fred hadn't heard or seen him approach. He shut off the car and pushed open the door.

"Are you trying to give me a heart attack?" he asked, willing his heart rate to return to normal.

Omar, standing over six feet tall with broad shoulders and dressed in all black, looked intimidating as hell. He stepped back as Fred climbed out of the vehicle.

"Sorry. Didn't mean to scare you. I heard you pull up, and when you didn't come into the house, I figured I'd check on you."

Omar was three years younger and a few inches taller and broader. His skin was a shade lighter than Fred's mocha tone, but they had the same dark eyes and full lips. Still, most people who saw them together didn't know right away that they were brothers.

"You all right?" Omar asked as he led the way into their house.

The three-bedroom bungalow was located on the east side of Atlanta in a neighborhood that was slowly being gentrified. A few years ago, they'd purchased the fixer-upper with the intent to renovate and flip it. Instead, they decided to live there while they worked on another property.

"Yeah, I'm fine. Just...just...." He shook his head and released a pent-up sigh. His heart rate had slowly gone back to normal, but Fred was still on edge.

Placing his keys on the kitchen counter, he moved past his brother and headed to the living room, where they had a partially stocked minibar to the right of the wall-mounted big-screen television. Nothing like some Jameson to calm his nerves. He poured himself three fingers of whiskey and turned to his brother, who had followed him into the room.

He held up the bottle. "Want some?"

Omar leaned on the back of the navy-blue leather recliner. "Nah, I'm good."

Fred took a large swig and closed his eyes, grimacing at the burn sliding down the back of his throat.

"Man, that's strong," he said, shaking his head.

Omar laughed. "Yeah, that stuff is not for the weak at heart. You probably should stick to your usual—light beer."

Fred chuckled and added a little more to his glass before carrying the tumbler to the leather sectional.

"Rough day?" Omar asked.

Fred grunted as he brought his drink up to his lips and sipped. He glanced over the rim at his brother. Omar was still in the sowing-his-wild-oats stage. Dressed in a black leather jacket, with a dark T-shirt and black jeans, Omar was obviously heading out to a club or a party—his usual Friday-night ritual.

"The day was okay. It was this evening that shook me up,

though. I took your advice and talked to the assistant district attorney overseeing the murder case."

Omar straightened, and his dark eyes grew large. "Seriously? How'd that go? Did you tell her everything?"

Fred picked up the television remote. "Yeah, I did. I hope I don't regret it."

"So, what's next? Did you agree to testify?"

"Yes. I'm just glad they've already arrested Dennis," he said, referring to the CEO of Leverage Construction Company.

On the night of the murder, Fred had suffered from being at the wrong place at the wrong time. As a custodial worker at a large office building, he'd been assigned to clean the Leverage Construction offices. That had led to the worst night of his life.

"How do you feel?" Omar asked.

"I'm tired as hell, but I'm glad I told the truth. Joyce was a nice lady. She was always kind to me, and I thought the least I could do was tell what had happened to her. I plan to do anything I can to help keep Mr. Stratton behind bars so he can pay for his crime. I'll just be glad when all of this is over."

"Well, I'm glad you told them the truth. I know it was eating at you. For what it's worth, I think you did the right thing." Omar strolled across the room to the coat closet. He grabbed his Yankees baseball cap and shoved it onto his head, pulling the brim low over his eyes. "What are your plans for the weekend?"

"Not much. I canceled my date with Raina. Now I'm just going to have another drink, jump in the shower, and hopefully sleep for the next two days."

If he had more personal days left at work, he'd use up every single one. At least his supervisor had reassigned him to a different floor, realizing he couldn't handle cleaning Leverage anymore—not without having nightmares. No one at work knew he had actually witnessed the murder. They only knew that he'd found the body, and Fred planned to keep it that way for as long as possible.

"Well, I'm out of here." Omar picked up his black duffel bag that Fred hadn't seen until now and looped it over his shoulder. "Heading to Suzanne's for the weekend. I'll check in on you, but holler if you need anything,"

Fred set his glass on the side table, then stretched out his legs and propped his size twelves on the table in front of him. "Will do. Have a good time."

Shortly after his brother left, Fred found himself dozing off, then jerking awake. He was so tired but trying to sleep the last few days only resulted in him waking up in a cold sweat. Even now, he kept remembering how the CEO had slammed the paperweight against the side of Joyce's head. It had been like watching a horror movie. Joyce's body crumbled to the floor, and she didn't get up. The vision played on a loop inside his head ever since that night.

Fred's eyes popped open when he thought he heard a noise coming from the kitchen. He bolted upright and listened. Seconds ticked by. Nothing.

Now, I'm hearing things.

He dropped back against the sofa and glanced at his watch. *Eleven-thirty*. He'd done more than doze. He had actually slept a few hours, but still, he was exhausted.

Heavy footsteps sounded against the hardwood floors, and Fred's gaze leaped toward the hallway that led to the bedrooms. Okay, maybe he wasn't crazy. His brother must've forgotten something.

"Omar?" Fred called out and started flipping through channels on the remote. "Man, you had me in here thinking that...."

A tall, imposing figure stepped into the room, and Fred leaped from the sofa, dropping the remote in the process. The person was dressed in all black, including the ski mask covering his face.

"What the.... Who the hell are—"

"You should've kept your mouth shut," the intruder said, his voice deep and raspy.

That's when Fred saw the large gun at the man's side.

His heart slammed against his chest, and an icy fear clawed through his body when the man raised his arm.

"No. No. Please...." Fred begged. He held his hands out in front of him as panic welled in his throat. He stumbled back, his leg making contact with the side table. "Please, please, don't...."

Chapter One

Journey collapsed on top of her husband's muscular chest, struggling to catch her breath as his intoxicating woodsy scent surrounded her. Despite the morning chorus of birds chirping outside their bedroom window, the house was fairly quiet. The only other sound was the rapid pace of her man's heartbeat against her ear. It matched the same staccato tempo of her own.

Morning sex was the best.

It didn't matter if it was a quickie; Lazarus Dimas had a way of putting it on her so thoroughly that each time he was inside of her felt like heaven. There might've been a couple of cracks in their marriage, but one thing was for sure, their love-making was still as intense as it had been the very first time their bodies joined.

It seemed like they'd been together forever, but it had only been a little over three years since they married. Journey couldn't imagine building a life with anyone else. Her love and desire for this strong, sexy man grew with each passing day. He and their almost-three-year-old daughter, Arielle, were everything to her.

Still panting, Laz placed a lingering kiss against her forehead, not caring about the beads of sweat littering her hairline.

"I'll never get enough of you," he murmured. His deep voice sent goosebumps racing over her heated skin, and the desire to go another round with him bloomed inside of her. "And this sexy body of yours...." His words trailed off as his large hands slid languidly down her back and didn't stop moving until he palmed her ass.

Journey's eyes drifted closed, and she moaned as he squeezed and kneaded her butt. She felt his erection growing again inside of her and rotated her hips as passion swirled within her.

"I see you're trying to get something else started, Detective Dimas."

Laz chuckled. He was no longer with Atlanta PD; now, he was a personal security specialist with Supreme Security, but she still called him *detective* from time to time.

He pulled her closer. "Like I said, I can't get enough of you."

Journey's eyes flew open, and she yelped when Laz flipped her onto her back. Then she burst out laughing. The man was big and strong and handled her as if she weighed nothing.

"Shhh...if you wake up Arielle...." he said, referring to their rambunctious daughter, "we won't have time to go another round."

He hovered above her, and Journey smiled while staring into his intense hazel-green eyes. Eyes that she had fallen in love with almost at first sight. He was such a handsome man. His Greek heritage was evident in his olive skin, which looked like he had spent all day in the sun, tanning his body to perfection.

She cupped his cheek, and her dark hand was such a contrast against his skin, like neon yellow paint against a black backdrop.

Journey slid her hands up into Laz's thick, black hair. He usually kept it short, but he had let it grow. Though it was hanging loose around his shoulders, he usually wore it in a short ponytail at the nape of his neck, intensifying his already badass persona.

"I love you," she said quietly as her fingers sifted through the soft strands.

Laz kissed her lips. "I love you, too." He trailed kisses over her jaw, near her ear, and worked his way down her neck.

There was so much Journey wanted to say to him.

Like...*I'm sorry*.

For the last few months, she'd been consumed by work. Her marriage had taken a back seat to her career—something Laz wasn't happy about. As an assistant district attorney, her schedule was unrelenting. It didn't help that she had recently been taking on more challenging cases, determined to win them and shine a favorable light on herself while she considered running for district attorney. She was just waiting for her boss to retire at the end of the year.

Too bad she didn't have Laz's support.

His gentle kisses down her body brought her back to the present and sent pleasure swirling inside her. Laz was the most amazing and supportive husband a woman could ever ask for. Until recently. She understood why he didn't want her to make a run for DA, especially since she kept canceling on him at every turn. Seemed everything lately was coming in second to her career.

Her husband was losing patience.

Her marriage was in jeopardy.

And it was all her fault.

I have to do better. I have to make some changes.

That's what she'd been telling herself, and she planned to start today. She looked forward to a much-needed family day hanging out with her husband and daughter.

Yes, her career meant everything to her, but nothing was more important than them.

Laz worked his way back up her body, peppering her skin with feathery kisses. "Why are you looking at me like that?" he asked when their gazes connected.

"What? I can't look at my smoking-hot husband?"

A wicked grin spread across his tempting lips. "Yeah, you can, but when you do, it makes me want you all over again."

Laz's mouth covered hers before she could respond. The kiss started slow and tender but soon turned more passionate as their tongues tangled. Heat soared through her, nipping at every nerve while their hands explored each other's naked bodies.

Their kiss deepened, and Journey whimpered into his mouth.

God, she loved this man more than life, and the thought squeezed her heart.

She couldn't lose Laz.

He was her everything.

A delicious shiver scurried over her skin when his hand went lower and moved between her legs. Her body was so tuned in to him, and everywhere Laz touched made it feel like fire seeping into her bones.

Journey gasped, and her back arched off the bed when the pad of his thumb made contact with her clit. She ripped her lips from his and closed her eyes tightly, the pleasure almost too much to handle.

Squirming beneath him, her head brushed back and forth against the pillow as Laz teased and caressed her sensitive bud.

The pressure continued to build inside her as he worked her body into a frenzy.

"La—Laz, babe...." she moaned and dug her nails into his skin, trying to hang on. When she looked at him, their gazes locked. "I want you inside me. I want.... Ohhhh...." She cried out when he slipped a finger inside her and then another.

His mouth covered hers, smothering the moans and whimpers she couldn't control. He continued wreaking intense havoc on her body, sending her arousal to another level. They'd just had a quickie, and Journey wanted this round to last, but....

"We want the same thing," he said, kissing her while moving his hand from between her legs. Gripping one of her thighs, Laz spread her wider and smoothly entered her.

Goodness. He was so long, thick, and hard. Laz filled her completely, and he went deeper and harder each time he pumped into her. Journey held on for the ride, picking up his rhythm and loving the way their bodies moved in perfect sync.

"Oh, yes." This was what she wanted. Him deep inside of her, rocking her body into submission. It wouldn't take much for her to have another orgasm, but she didn't want to come yet. She wanted to prolong the intense sensation spinning inside of her and threatening to push her to her release.

Laz watched her with lowered lashes and drove into her with more force as he stared down at her. "You know I can't handle it when your tits bounce up and down like that," he growled.

Journey started to laugh, but it came out as a whimper. "I—I can't help it when you move in and out of me like...like.... Ohhhhh, yes."

His mouth suddenly covering her nipple took her to new heights. The combination of his masterful tongue loving on her breasts and his continued pumping into her pushed her closer to no return.

He lifted his head. "You feel so damn good," he ground out, and his hips moved faster. He went deeper and harder, each stroke getting her closer to....

"Yes! Oh yes, Laz!" she cried out. He quickly covered her mouth with his, smothering her screams. All the while, he continued thrusting in and out of her until his own release threw him over the edge of control.

His body stiffened, then shook before he collapsed on top of her. His heavy breathing mingled with hers, and Journey wrapped her arms around him. Once again, she struggled to catch her breath.

Yep, she loved morning quickies.

"You never cease to wear my ass out," Laz panted and dropped onto his back. After a couple of deep breaths, he pulled her to his side and kissed the top of her head. "If we didn't already have plans for family day, I'd suggest we spend the day in bed," he said.

Energy spent, Journey snuggled against him and draped her arm and one of her legs across his body. "That would be nice, but we promised Ashton and Dani that we'd be at the celebration," she reminded him. "I still can't believe the adoption went through so quickly."

"Yeah, Ashton is beyond happy," Laz said sleepily and tightened his arm around Journey.

Their friends, Ashton Chambers and his wife Dani had just adopted two children. Not just any children either. Months ago, right before Ashton left the police force, one of his confidential informants was brutally murdered, and he felt responsible.

The murdered woman left behind an eighteen-year-old son, a five-year-old son, and a little girl who had just turned three. The oldest had already joined the army, and their grandmother had initially been awarded custody of the younger children. Since she could not properly care for them, Ashton and Dani stepped in. The adoption was finalized two days ago, and today friends and family were meeting up to help celebrate.

"I'm glad you took the day off," Laz murmured. "We need some family time."

"I know, and I'm sorry I've been bailing on you and Arielle. But I knew I had to take today off, especially with Arielle and my parents leaving for Florida tomorrow. I wanted to make sure we spent the day with her," Journeys said.

Their daughter was so excited about going to Disney World with her grandparents. It was all she'd been talking about for the last few weeks.

"If it weren't for your dad being a former detective, I wouldn't feel comfortable with her going. You know that, right? She's still just a baby," Laz said.

"I'm glad you finally came around, but she'll be three in a couple of weeks. She's not a baby anymore."

"She's my baby," he grumbled, sounding like he was about to fall asleep. "You both are. Which is why I need you around more. No more putting work before us. Agreed?"

Journey tilted her head back and smiled at him. His sleepy gaze met hers. "Agreed. I'm going to do better. I promise," she said, meaning it. No longer would she take her marriage for granted.

She reached up and kissed him, but they were interrupted when her cell phone rang.

Laz stiffened, and Journey had to keep herself from groaning at the familiar ringtone.

"Don't answer it," Laz said with an edge in his tone.

The screen flashed Prentice Johnson, an investigator for the DA's office and Journey's go-to person on the majority of her cases. She considered him a partner, and they were currently working on a case that was proving to be more complicated than she initially thought. But she needed to win it to keep her winning streak alive. She had won twenty-seven out of her last thirty cases, and that was going to look good on her record if she ran for DA.

The phone rang again, and Journey huffed out a breath. "I'm sorry, babe, but I have to get this."

Before she could grab her cell from the nightstand, Laz jerked out of bed and headed to the bathroom.

"Tell that asshole to never call my house on a Saturday morning again," he growled and slammed the bathroom door.

Journey flinched even though she saw it coming, then she answered the phone.

"Your timing *sucks*."

Chapter Two

Laz stood on the other side of the kitchen island and stared at Journey. Clearly, he had heard her wrong. That had to be it because there was no way she would cancel their plans.

"What the hell do you mean, you have to go to work? Journey, we just talked about this. It's family day. We both agreed to take the day off!"

"Shh, keep your voice down," she murmured and glanced into the family room where Arielle was watching cartoons. "It's only for a few minutes. An hour, tops. I have to do—"

"Fuck that." Laz stabbed a finger in her direction. "You don't have to do shit. You—"

"Be mad all you want, but don't you *dare* curse at me!" she snapped, only loud enough for him to hear, then closed the gap between them. "There are some parts of my job that I can't just turn off. You know that."

He tried to never disrespect her, or talk to her in a way that was brazen, but he was struggling to keep his anger at bay.

Every damn week *and* weekend, she gave one excuse after another for why she couldn't do something that involved him and their daughter.

He was sick of it.

Sick of her canceling outings.

Sick of her calling him in a panic when she couldn't pick Arielle up from daycare on time.

And sick of her putting him last.

He couldn't keep doing this. She either wanted to be married—or she didn't.

"Babe, I'm sorry," she said. "I know it seems like I'm always putting you and Arielle last."

"Because you are, Journey," he seethed. "You're the smartest woman I know. How is it that you can't see that?"

Her gaze dropped to the floor, and he watched her as she nibbled on her bottom lip, struggling for something to say. Laz's heart clenched as disappointment engulfed him. It seemed as if he and Arielle didn't matter to her.

When they married and promised to love each other until the end of time, he meant it. He meant every word of his vows, and no one could ever say he wasn't living up to that commitment. And though Journey had never planned to get married, Laz believed she had meant her vows, too. Granted, one of the reasons they'd married was because she'd gotten pregnant, but the number-one reason was because they loved each other.

Her actions lately had him doubting everything. There wasn't much that frightened him. Yet, the idea of losing his wife or having to walk away from their marriage scared him to death.

His gaze traveled the length of her. Journey was such an amazing woman—beautiful inside and out, intelligent, and sexy as hell. Her hair hung loose in big curls, and though she didn't need makeup, it was applied flawlessly.

When it came to work, she never stepped out of the house without looking totally pulled together. Today was no different. She was wearing the hell out of a navy-blue suit. The jacket molded over her full breasts and tapered in to show off a narrow waist. The slim-fitting skirt stopped just above her knees and revealed the best pair of shapely legs he'd ever seen on a woman. They were accentuated by the high heels that matched her suit.

When his buddies teased him about marrying up, Laz couldn't even argue that fact because it was true. Journey was everything he thought he'd never be able to have. With his bad-boy rep around the city, no one was more surprised than him when they'd started dating. Especially since she had once told him that she wasn't ever getting married. It just wasn't something she had planned for her future.

But getting married and settling down with one special woman had been important to him. He'd been engaged years before meeting Journey, but his fiancée at the time had been murdered. He never thought his heart would recover from that, but then Journey came along.

They were as different as apples and broccoli, which had been extremely evident when they first met. Laz had been a detective with Atlanta PD, and she was a prosecutor. Where she followed the law to a T, he skated on the edge of it, pushing boundaries left and right to put as many bad guys behind bars as possible. She was sweet and kind. He was tough and brash at times.

By all accounts, they shouldn't have been attracted to each other, but fate stepped in. Now Laz physically ached, knowing that they were drifting apart.

Journey huffed out a breath. "Do you think I like canceling on you and my daughter or disappointing you? I don't. You should know that it has to be extenuating circumstances to make me do that to the two most important people in my life."

Laz turned away and pulled down a travel mug from one of the upper cabinets. Then poured coffee into it. "Quit lawyering me, Journey. Save your closing statements for the courtroom. I've heard this all before. Yet, here we are again—you canceling plans."

"This case has hit one brick wall after another, and I was losing hope. But a witness has come forward. I have to talk to her today, Laz. You know how important it is to speak to them as soon as possible."

As a former detective, yes, he knew better than anyone the importance of hooking a witness. That still didn't mean he liked her putting work first.

"I promise it won't take long."

"Right now, Journey, your promises don't mean a damn thing. Last month, you promised to attend your sister's barbecue. Last Sunday—your day off—you promised dinner out with me. And less than an hour ago, you promised that you were going with us to the celebration. What am I supposed to tell Ashton and Dani?"

"You act like I'm not going to the celebration. I'm just going to be a little late. Why are you tripping?" Journey's phone vibrated, and she glanced at the screen. "Okay, Prentice is outside. After I say bye to Arielle I—"

"You spend an awful lot of time with your investigator. Are you fucking him?"

Journey reared back as if she'd been slapped. Her wide eyes and shocked expression quickly turned into anger as she got in Laz's face. He towered over her by several inches, but she was one person who wasn't intimidated by him. His little spitfire never took shit from him, one of many things he loved about her.

"Are you seriously asking me that?" She glowered at him. If looks could kill, he'd be six feet under without her even having to lay a finger on him.

Laz didn't respond. He hated that he even went there, but the words left his mouth before he could stop them. He knew Journey would never step out on him. Not because he'd kill any man who dared put his hands on her, but because deep down, he knew she loved him.

At least that's what he wanted to believe.

Laz released a long breath and brushed his hand over his mouth and beard.

"You know what? Do whatever the hell you want."

Journey placed her hands on his chest before he could walk away, and a lightning bolt of electricity shot through him from his head to his feet. It never failed. She had such a visceral effect on him, even when he was pissed at her.

"Babe, what has gotten into you?" she asked, concern and confusion flashing in her dark, pretty eyes. "I know I've been flaking on you lately, but it won't always be like this. You know that."

Laz stepped out of her reach and leaned against the counter. "Jay, there's going to always be a case that you need to pour your all into, and I understand that—to a point. If it's like this now, how is it going to be if you become DA? I'm not going to keep waiting on the sideline until you decide to put Arielle and me first."

"What are you saying?" she asked, and her voice held a slight tremble.

Laz had never loved another human being the way he loved her, and he believed in his heart that the feelings were mutual. But at what point should he say enough?

"Just once, I'd love for you to put me first." He headed out of the kitchen. "Have fun at work."

"Laz, please...."

He walked out of the room without looking back. Part of him wanted to fight for his marriage and do whatever was necessary to make things right between them. But the other part of him wanted to just say *fuck it*—and move on.

Right now, he wasn't sure which part of him would win.

Chapter Three

"I think you're being too hard on your wife."

Laz glared at Hamilton Crosby—his best friend and the managing partner of Supreme Security, where Laz worked as a personal security specialist. Technically, Ham was also his boss. The two of them were camped out in the party room, along with Ashton, who was holding his sleeping daughter. Ashton and Dani had decided to have the party at an indoor trampoline park that seemed to have a hundred different types of trampolines for all ages and sizes.

"Did I ask for your opinion?" Laz grabbed another slice of pizza and sat across from the two guys.

For the past couple of hours, the three of them, along with some of the other guys from Supreme, had been on kid duty but managed to talk a little about Laz's situation. They were taking a break while a few others, including some of the wives, were with the kids.

All except his wife.

Journey had texted and left a couple of voicemails letting him know that she might not make it to the party. He had already known that was going to happen, proving that her work was her top priority.

"You didn't have to ask my opinion," Hamilton said. "But that's never stopped me from giving it. Take it from a husband who also has a feisty, strong-willed, incredible woman sharing his household. Let Journey do her job, and just keep supporting her. You already know she's worth the effort."

Laz did know, but that didn't make him feel any better. He also wasn't sure how much more he could take.

"He's right," Ashton added as he rocked his little girl.

Ashton was one of Laz's best friends. They'd been detectives and partners at Atlanta PD for years, and now they were both security specialists.

Laz couldn't be happier for Ashton. Coming from a large family, he had always wanted a wife and kids. Now he had both. He'd married a bar owner, Dani, ten months ago, and now they were parents of a five-year-old, Caulder, and a three-year-old, Tabitha.

His friend finally had the family he wanted. But that didn't mean he knew enough about marriage to agree with Hamilton.

"I know you're not trying to give me marriage advice," Laz said to Ashton, trying to add mock annoyance to his tone. "You've been married for a whole two minutes. You don't know shit yet."

He flinched when Ashton narrowed his eyes and nodded down at Tabitha. She might've been asleep, but Laz did need to work on the cursing, especially since he was around kids all the time.

"Just wait until Dani starts giving you a hard time," Laz added around a mouthful of pizza. "Then we'll see who needs the advice."

Ashton burst out laughing but quieted when Tabitha stirred. "Do you know my wife?" he said. "She's been giving me a hard time since the day I set foot in her bar. Trust me, I don't have to be married for years to know that we're all with the type of women who will do whatever the heck they want to do. That is probably why we fell in love with them in the first place.

"They're not pushovers. They go the extra mile for people or causes they believe in. And more than anything, no matter how busy or distracted they are, they love us." Ashton stood while cradling his daughter. "Besides, you knew how demanding Journey's job was before you married her. So, stop complaining and give her some grace. Now, if you will excuse me, I'm going to go find my wife."

"For a person who's only been married a minute, I think he nailed that advice," Hamilton said. His lips were twitching as if trying to keep a straight face. "But seriously...are you and Journey all right?"

Laz finished his pizza and wiped his mouth. "I don't know, man. In some ways, our relationship is amazing," he said, thinking about their lovemaking that morning. "But I don't like that she's obsessed with this job, and everything else, including Arielle and me, comes last. I especially don't like that she thinks nothing about canceling on me."

"We both know that it's not intentional," Hamilton said, leaning back in his chair. He crossed his arms. "I know that Journey would do anything for you and Arielle. Maybe she's having a hard time juggling all of her responsibilities. Just give her a little time."

"Time?" Laz snapped and jerked out of his seat. He ran his hand over his head in frustration. "This shit has been going on for months. I can't count on her, Ham, and that's what's bothering me. I used to always be able to count on my wife for anything."

Laz snapped his mouth shut when Kenton Bailey and

Angelo González walked in. They both pulled up short and looked from him to Hamilton.

"Are we interrupting something?" Kenton asked.

Most of the Supreme personal security specialists had a military background or were former law enforcement, which was why the team was often referred to as *Atlanta's Finest*. Hamilton was an ex-cop who Laz used to work with early in his career. Kenton, a former FBI agent, might've been the biggest guy on the team, but he was a gentle giant with a great sense of humor. Angelo used to be an undercover agent for the DEA, but he should've pursued a singing career like his former superstar wife, Zenobia. The man could give the singer Usher some competition.

"Nah, I was just leaving to go and check on Ari," Laz said, knowing he wasn't fooling either of them. Especially if the way the side-eye Kenton was shooting at him was any indication.

Laz didn't want anyone in his business. It wasn't that he didn't trust and respect them, because he did, which was saying a lot because he didn't trust easily. He was fairly sure they already suspected something was up with him and Journey. All of their families often got together, and Journey had missed plenty of the gatherings lately.

He cringed when he stepped out of the room and closed the door behind him. The noise level was off the charts, even in the eating area. The building was huge with tons of trampoline apparatuses and kids everywhere he looked. That included his daughter, who was running toward him with Dakota, Hamilton's wife, hot on her heels.

"Daddy!" Arielle screamed, joy showing on her cute face.

Laz's heart turned over in his chest every time he looked at her.

He might be biased, but their daughter was the most beautiful child he'd ever laid eyes on. She had a little of both of their features and temperament. Her interracial heritage was evident in her skin tone—coffee with a lot of cream. She had his hazel-green eyes, thick wavy hair, and his ability to size a person up within seconds. Even at her age, she could spot bullshit from a mile away. She was a cutie-pie like her mother and had Journey's nose, mouth, and smile.

Unfortunately, she was stubborn as hell...like the both of them. Her strong will challenged him and Journey on a daily basis. Still, he loved his baby to death.

"Hi, Daddy!" she squealed as if she hadn't seen him in a long time when it had only been minutes. She slammed into him, and her arms went around one of his legs.

"Hey, baby girl. Are you having fun?" He lifted her into his arms and buried his nose in the crook of her neck, inhaling her fresh baby scent while sending her into a fit of giggles.

God, he loved this kid. She was his heart.

"Stop, Daddy." Still laughing, she wiggled in his hold.

Laz stopped the torture and placed a kiss on her soft cheek. "Are you having fun?"

She nodded her head, and her two long ponytails bobbed back and forth on each side of her head. "I'm being a good listener."

"I'm glad to hear that you're being a good listener for Auntie Dee, Dani, and Zen."

She'd been pretty proud of herself the last few months since her preschool teacher gave out stickers to good listeners. They chatted for a few minutes before Ashton's son Caulder ran over with Dylan, Hamilton's youngest son. He and Arielle were born months apart and were best of friends.

Arielle pushed against Laz's chest and wiggled against him.

"Down, Daddy. Down," she said, struggling to get out of his hold.

The moment Laz set her on her feet, the three took off,

running back to the trampoline area. He started to follow, wanting to make sure they were supervised, but Dakota waved him off, letting him know that she had them.

Laz huffed out a breath. Looked like he'd be there for a while longer.

An hour later, Laz and Arielle were finally leaving, and he couldn't have been happier. As he stepped outside the building, his ears were still ringing from the noise inside, but all that mattered was that the kids had a good time. He and Arielle were the first to leave, but the others would probably soon follow.

Laz gripped Arielle's hand tighter as he slipped on his shades with his other hand. He was hoping the trampoline park would've worn her out, but the way she was skipping along beside him said otherwise.

"We go home?" she asked.

"Not yet, sweetie." He was thinking about taking her to the Humane Society to look at puppies, something she enjoyed doing. He just wished Journey was going with them.

In her last voice message, apologizing for not being there with them, she promised to make it up to him and Arielle tonight. It didn't matter. It was the fact that she bailed on them in the first place that bothered him.

"I—I wanna go home, Daddy. Grandma's looking for me. I'm going to see Princess Tiana."

Laz smiled. He loved that she was excited about her trip to Florida with Journey's parents, even if he didn't want to let her go. He gently tugged on one of her ponytails and smiled again when she started giggling.

"You're not going with them until tomorrow. Today you're all mine." Laz still wasn't comfortable with her being away from him for a whole week, but he knew she would have a blast at Disney World.

"I was a good listener today," Arielle announced cheerfully.

Laz chuckled. He wondered how long he and Journey would have to hear how good of a listener she was.

Laz strolled through the small parking lot before moving to the sidewalk. Since the lot had been full, he'd had to park on the street earlier.

His grip on Arielle's small hand tightened when his SUV came into sight, but that wasn't what gave him pause.

It was the shady-looking guys, four of them, hanging near the truck that suddenly had his pulse pounding loudly in his ears.

Shit. What the hell are they up to?

Chapter Four

As a detective, Laz had witnessed the scene many times Immediately, he went on alert. The punks were getting ready to make an exchange if the way they kept glancing around was any indication. As soon as the thought filtered into his mind, two of them went on watch while the other two exchanged money and a couple of small packets.

A wave of unease crept through Laz, and he maintained a firm grip on Arielle's hand as he discreetly glanced around.

The punks did it smoothly enough, but it bothered him that they were doing this in broad daylight. That meant they didn't care much if anyone saw them. Only a few cars were driving by periodically, and Laz noticed a handful of people going in and out of some of the businesses across the street. No one appeared to be paying them any mind.

Except for him.

"I wanna go, Daddy," Arielle said, looking up at him with innocent eyes.

"Okay, one second."

Laz picked her up into his arms, despite her protests. He debated taking her back into the building because he'd seen enough of these exchanges to know they could quickly turn violent. All it would take was for one of the guys to get mad at not receiving enough money or one to find something wrong with the product.

Laz had seen it all. Too many times, the situation didn't end well.

Before he could return to the building, the guys dispersed. Two walked in the opposite direction, away from him, and the other two started across the street, talking it up as if nothing had happened. One of them glanced his way, but it was quick as the man continued laughing with his buddy.

"Daddy?" Arielle's questioning tone snagged Laz's attention.

"Okay, let's get going," he said and started for his SUV again.

"Laz! Hey, Laz, wait up." Someone called out from behind him just before he reached the truck.

Laz glanced over his shoulder and saw a man in his mid-twenties jogging toward him. He slid his sunglasses down his nose and peeked over the top of them. It wasn't until the guy got closer that Laz recognized him.

"Nazir? Dude, it's been a long time," Laz greeted. He shifted Arielle in his arms and gave the man a fist bump.

The former drug addict appeared to have finally gotten his act together. His tawny brown complexion gleamed under the sunlight, and his dark eyes held a bit of humor. So used to seeing the guy with red-rimmed eyes, Laz was a little taken back.

Today, Nazir looked like a new man with his hair cut low and tight on the sides, and he was clean-shaven, giving him a boyish look. Gone were the ratty clothes that he used to walk around in for days at a time. Clearly, that was no longer the case. He was neatly dressed in a long-sleeve T-shirt with a local restaurant logo in the upper left-hand corner. The name-brand jeans and a pair of the latest Nikes told Laz that the kid had cleaned up well.

"What do you think?" Nazir lifted his arms and turned back and forth. "I've been clean for forty-eight months, two weeks, and three days," he said with a laugh. "Basically, over four years, and that's all thanks to you."

They had first met about five years ago when Laz busted him for disorderly conduct. After a few more encounters and arrests, Laz had helped him get into a drug treatment center.

Laz slipped his sunglasses on top of his head. "Nah, man. Don't give me the credit. You're the one who did the work, and it looks like it paid off."

"It did, and I ain't gonna lie, it was hard," he said with a chuckle and smiled at Arielle. "Hey, cutie."

Arielle gave a little wave, then laid her head on Laz's shoulder. She was shy at first meeting people, but she usually warmed up quickly.

"Is she yours?" Nazir asked, and Laz nodded. "She's beautiful. She must take after her mother." He burst out laughing, and Laz joined in.

"Yeah, you're making jokes, but it's actually true," Laz said and smiled down at Arielle. The February temperature was warmer than usual, but there was a strong breeze, and he pulled her lightweight jacket closed.

"Walk with me to my truck and tell me what's been going on," Laz said. "I have to get out of here, but I have a few minutes to talk."

As they strolled to the SUV, Laz listened as Nazir told him that after going to rehab the first time, he fell back into bad habits. Getting clean from any addiction wasn't easy, and listening to the kid proved that. His family had given up on him, and his mother, a single parent, regrettably had to kick him out of the house.

"Things got worse before they got better," Nazir said. "It took me three stints in rehab to get to this point."

"I'm glad to hear you didn't give up," Laz said.

When they reached his truck, he used the keyless entry to disarm it. He had purchased the vehicle the day after Arielle was born, wanting to ensure he had something safe and dependable to drive her around in.

He opened the back passenger door and placed Arielle in the car seat.

"No, Daddy. I do it," Arielle insisted when Laz started to buckle her up. She could do it herself, but it usually took longer than he had time for. "I do it," she said again with authority, pushing his hand away.

"Okay, but if you don't have it fastened by the time I get in the truck, I'm going to fasten it. So, hurry up." Laz kept her door open to keep an eye on her while he and Nazir talked for a few more minutes.

The kid sounded proud of himself, as he should. Kicking a bad habit with the support of family and friends was hard, but it was even harder when you had to rely mostly on yourself.

"Daddy, almost," Arielle said, still fiddling with the buckle.

Shaking his head, Laz smiled, and Nazir chuckled.

"Little Miss Independent is not giving up," Nazir cracked.

"No, and she won't. She's a determined kid." Laz moved to the door opening to see Arielle's progress. She must've thought he was going to take over because she quickly told him she could do it. "Okay, but remember, if you're not done by the time I get in, I will do it."

"'kay," she said, still struggling to latch the buckle.

Laz closed the door, and he and Nazir continued talking as they moved around the back of the vehicle to the driver's side.

"Do you need a ride?" Laz asked as an afterthought as he pulled open the front door of the truck.

"No, but thanks. I work at the Greek restaurant across the street." Nazir nodded toward the large building at the other end of the corner. "My shift starts in a little while, so I should probably get going, but I'm glad I ran into you. It gives me a chance to say thanks. If it weren't for you, I probably would still be living on the street or worse."

"I'm glad I could help, and I...." Laz's words trailed off when he spotted a dark sedan with tinted windows pull out of a parking spot down the street. It wouldn't have been a big deal if the car wasn't creeping along at a snail's pace.

Nazir turned to see what he was looking at, then turned back to Laz. "Same ol' Laz. Some things never change. You're always on guard," the kid was saying, but Laz's focus was on the vehicle.

The car hadn't sped up. Maybe the driver was looking for an address, but Laz's intuition had never failed him, and right now, his gut was starting to swirl. He suddenly wanted to get the hell out of there.

His gaze took in every nearby person, which wasn't many. The two-lane road wasn't that busy, but there were a few people out and about, coming and going from some of the storefront businesses across the street.

Still, something felt off.

"Nazir, it was great seeing you," Laz said but kept his attention on the car. "You probably should get going so you don't be late."

"Oh, yeah, that's right." Nazir glanced at the watch on his left wrist. "I better get going."

Tires squealed, and Laz whipped his head to the right, just

in time to see the same car flying up the street. Then it slowed down a few yards away, and unease clawed through him.

His body moved without thought. He bent down and pulled his pistol from his ankle holster before taking a couple of cautious steps back to where he had left his car door open.

This could be nothing, but....

"Arielle, get on the floor!"

"Daddy...."

"Fall on the floor, now, Ari! Hurry! Nazir, get out of here. No, get down!"

"Laz, man...."

The sedan's tinted windows rolled down, and the moment Laz spotted a gun barrel, he dove to the ground. Before he could form his next thought, gunshots blasted through the air, hitting nearby vehicles and his truck.

Shit!

Screams rang out, and he heard feet pounding the pavement, but there was only one voice that penetrated Laz's brain.

Arielle.

"Daddy!" she screamed over and over. "Daddy!"

"Stay down, Ari!" he yelled from the ground and turned slightly, able to get off a couple of shots, hitting the side of the car. "Stay down, baby!"

Nazir gasped and crumbled to the asphalt holding his chest. Blood spilled through his fingers, and fear like nothing Laz had ever experienced gripped him.

He had to get to his kid. She was screaming for him.

Everything was happening so fast. Laz returned fire while trying to take cover, but cursed when a bullet whizzed by and pinged off his truck.

One of the windows shattered. Then another.

Arielle.

Laz had to get to her.

Needing to get to the other side of the truck, he fired off several rounds while he lifted himself up, planning to make a run for it. A bullet slammed into his shoulder, knocking him against the truck.

He cried out as hot, searing pain stabbed him in the shoulder and traveled down his arm.

His gun slipped from his grip when he crashed to the ground.

More bullets flew, and he flinched when one kicked up rocks near his head. He had to move and under the truck was his only option.

He dragged himself beneath the vehicle with his good arm, but each move he made brought with it a stabbing pain that stole his breath.

Don't stop.

Don't stop.

Keep moving.

Arielle needed him.

Yelling and people running could be heard in the distance. Bullets were still whizzing by, but Laz blocked out everything except the need to get to his child. He couldn't move fast. Not only was his wound fighting against him, but the truck's undercarriage wasn't as high as he needed. He kept getting snagged but eventually made it to the other side.

Dammit.

He was parked too close to the curb. He couldn't get on the sidewalk and had to belly-crawl with one arm to the rear of the vehicle. Just as he started to pull up on the sidewalk, the car peeled away, but Arielle was still screaming.

Laz didn't know what was worse, the searing pain that left his arm immobile or the fear that his daughter was hurt.

On his knees and with strength he didn't know he had, he

wrenched open the back door and found his baby on the floor with her hands over her ears.

Relief flooded through him, and emotion clogged his throat as tears filled his eyes. He blinked them away, ignoring how his chest tightened at seeing her.

"Come here, baby," he said, dizziness clouding his vision. He blinked rapidly, trying to focus but staggered and bumped into the truck door. Only sheer will kept him upright. "Co—come here."

Still crying uncontrollably, Arielle crawled toward him, falling on her face once when her arms gave out, but she kept moving until she reached the door.

Emotion gripped Laz when she touched his hand, and a tear slipped down his cheek. He didn't give a damn. He just needed to hold her.

"Daddy," Arielle cried, sniffing hard enough to shake her little body. She frantically clawed at his clothes and pulled herself onto his body.

She might've been tiny, but the way she lunged at him, the momentum and her weight sent him crashing backward, and he fell to the sidewalk. But he didn't let go of her. He held her close and was able to lean against the edge of the door.

"Are you hurt?" Laz asked.

She had stopped screaming but was still whimpering and sniffling. He needed to check her, but the death grip she had around his neck made it almost impossible. That and the fact that he was seeing double as dizziness rocked him. Still, he ran his good hand down her body, praying that he wouldn't feel any blood.

She seemed okay, but he wasn't sure as he struggled to keep his head up. His eyes drifted closed despite willing himself to stay alert.

Yelling and footsteps reached his ears, and he held Arielle as tight as he could. He'd die protecting her.

"Laz! Laz!"

"You two stay with him."

"Partial plate."

"Angelo is chasing after the car on foot."

Relief flooded through Laz, knowing that his guys were there. Everyone talked at once. He opened his eyes, but his world was spinning. All he could do was hold onto his baby.

"Laz? Dammit. It looks like he took at least one to the shoulder," someone said.

"EMTs are on their way," came another voice.

Laz jerked and almost lost it when someone put their hands on him and tried to pry Arielle out of his arms. She started screaming, burying her face into his neck, and he felt her hot tears against his skin.

Laz held her tighter.

"No!" he yelled, but he didn't hear his own voice. "No," he said again.

"Come on, Laz, it's Ham. You gotta let her go so I can check you both out."

"No," Laz bit out. Pain along the left side of his body had him gritting his teeth when a somewhat blurry Hamilton came into view.

"Laz, you gotta work with me, man. Let Arielle go."

"I can't." Laz felt himself fading. He couldn't hang on. "My wife...Journey. I need...her."

That was his last thought before everything faded to black.

Chapter Five

Journey gripped the car door handle. The once-steady beat of her heart had ratcheted up a hundred percent as she watched the coroner load the black body bag into the back of their van.

How could this have happened? She had just met with Fred, and now....

"I can't believe he's dead," she whispered into the quietness of Prentice's car. They were sitting in his Ford Taurus, staring out the windshield. Law enforcement had come in heavy. Though some had already left, the detectives on the case and medical examiner were still on the scene.

"As of yesterday, Fred was our key witness. Now, he's gone. This case is falling apart, and that low-down dirty murderer might walk."

Journey knew she was being a little dramatic, but deep down, she was concerned. They only had circumstantial evidence against the CEO, Dennis Stratton, and considering the defense team he'd hired, Journey would have to bring her A-game. She couldn't walk into that courtroom in the coming weeks or months with what little they had and expect a victory. They needed to build a stronger case if she had any hopes of winning.

"Don't worry. Fred might've been a key witness, but he's not the only one," Prentice said, removing his tan newsboy cap and setting it on the center console. As he stared down at his cell phone, he rubbed his bald head, something he often did when deep in thought.

"Well, we know one thing," Journey said. "Since the CEO is behind bars, he couldn't have killed this guy."

"That doesn't mean that he didn't have him killed," Prentice said, drinking coffee he'd been nursing for the last couple of hours. No doubt it was cold by now.

"That's true," Journey conceded, wondering what this would do to her case.

When authorities called them about Fred's murder, saying that he'd been killed sometime around eleven p.m. the night before, she and Prentice had just met with Marta Polczynski. So far, Journey wasn't sure she could use the woman as a witness even though she was one of the three accountants who worked at Leverage Construction.

Marta was holding something back. Journey wasn't positive, but she'd been interviewing witnesses a long time, and she would bet that the accountant knew more than she was letting on.

Journey just didn't know what.

Marta wanted them to believe that Leverage Construction was the perfect place to work, where employees were treated like family, and everyone got along great. It was possible that was the case, but it was her overly-cheerful demeanor that hadn't sat well with Journey.

How could anyone be cheerful when a coworker was recently murdered where they worked? Yet, not once did

Marta express any empathy, ask questions regarding what happened the night of the murder, the fate of the CEO, or even show any concern for her own safety. It was almost as if someone had gotten to her.

Had she been threatened? Or was she somehow involved in the murder?

From what the DA's office knew, she wasn't involved. If not that, maybe this was how she handled traumatic situations. If it was, it was the opposite of her coworkers who'd been questioned. Those people had clearly been grieving, and they showed sympathy for Joyce's family and even the construction company as a whole.

Journey couldn't stop wondering—was Marta involved in the murder somehow?

Hopefully, the woman would be like Fred and eventually come forward and tell them everything she knew. If not, Journey planned to take another go at her.

"Yes!" Prentice said, jarring Journey out of her thoughts. "Joyce's husband is willing to talk to me again. Should I see if he's available now since he might be able to add something to the case?"

Journey nibbled on her bottom lip as she contemplated whether to try and question the guy today. She had already ruined family day, but she was hoping to make up for it by being home when Laz and Arielle arrived.

She sighed and stared out the window, noting how law enforcement vehicles had mostly cleared out. Now would be a perfect time to chat with the victim's husband. Maybe he could shed more light on Joyce's role with the company and whether she was having any trouble with anyone on staff. When they'd first questioned him, he'd been so distraught he was in no condition to answer many of their questions.

"Journey?" Prentice said.

"Oh, I'm sorry. Either you can meet with him alone today, or we both can meet with him Monday morning. But right now, I need to get home."

She first needed to stop and pick up dinner from Laz's favorite restaurant. She also needed to make a few more stops to add to her apology tonight.

"Monday it is. I'll drop you off at home, then give him a call." Prentice started the car and pulled away from the curb. "Speaking of home, did you tell your hot-headed husband that someone threatened you?"

"If I had, I wouldn't be in a car sitting next to you. He would've become my shadow. Then again, he might not care," she mumbled, then regretted her last words.

Laz wasn't the most patient person in the world and was often quick to react, but his parting words to her that morning were so unlike him. He had raised his voice at her a few times in the past when they had heated discussions, but nothing like this morning.

"Ahh. Well, it doesn't take my A-1 investigation skills to recognize when there's trouble in paradise. Want to talk about it?" Prentice asked as he split his attention between her and the road.

"Not really...except I think Laz is going to leave me."

Silence fell between them before Prentice burst out laughing. He glanced at her and then back to the street, still snickering.

Journey glared at him as hurt crept through her body. "There was nothing funny about anything I just said," she bit out, suddenly wanting to punch him and take all her frustration out on him. "Or do you get off on people telling you that their marriage might be over?"

He dabbed at the corners of his eyes with the heel of his hand. "I'm sorry. It's just that...if it was any other couple, I might be concerned. But you and Laz? Journey, you two are so in love and perfect for each other, it's nauseating. There is no way in hell Laz would ever leave you." He shook his head. "No way. I'm not buying it. You forget...I know him."

He and Laz had worked for the same precinct for a while when Prentice was a detective with Atlanta PD. That was before moving over to the DA's office and becoming an investigator.

Prentice stopped at a red light. "Journey, Laz would walk through fire for you. Hell, he already has...sorta," he said.

Journey knew he was referring to the time she'd been kidnapped. Not too many people knew about that, and thankfully it had never made it to the media. But from what she'd been told, when Laz found out she was missing, he lost it. Hunted the city tirelessly for her and had even pulled his gun on folks, trying to get answers. He hadn't literally walked through fire, but there was no doubt that he would've if he had to.

When the light changed, Prentice pulled off. "No offense, but everybody knows your husband can be an asshole on most days. With that said, though, I have mad respect for the way that man worships you. I'm telling you, unless you've done something suicidal like cheat on him, I doubt you have anything to worry about. Besides, I know you would never step out on him."

Journey stared out of the passenger window, remembering how Laz had made the off-handed comment about her having an affair with Prentice. She knew he didn't believe it, but the fact that he had even spoken the words meant her marriage—more importantly, their relationship—was in trouble.

"A lot has changed over the last couple of months," she said to Prentice. "You know I've been taking on our biggest cases, trying to show how dedicated I am to this office. I want that

DA's position when Henry retires," she said of her boss, Henry Gaines. "But my marriage is more important than my career. If I'm struggling to juggle the two now, I don't know if I can handle a more demanding job."

"I get that you're eyeing the DA's position, but maybe just focus on the here and now. When the time comes, you'll know if it's something you should pursue. Now, getting back to my original question. Why didn't you tell Laz about the threat?"

"You know better than anyone how many threats prosecutors and defense attorneys receive." She shrugged. "It's just a part of the job. Besides, I think it's a scare tactic, probably from someone who works for Leverage Construction. When Dennis Stratton's defense attorney made that public statement, sounding like the company would collapse without him, his employees probably got nervous."

"Yeah, I thought that was interesting. It's a multimillion-dollar corporation. I can't see it falling apart just because he's not in charge."

"Yeah, me either. I doubt the board of directors or any of the executives would let that happen. It's not like he founded the company. So, I think one of the employees or...." she shrugged, "...somebody is pissed that the CEO was arrested."

She hated when their office received threats, and if they fell apart or freaked out every time someone wanted them to drop a case, they wouldn't ever lock up the bad guys.

"Is that the only reason you didn't tell Laz about the threat?"

Journey dropped her head against the headrest. "Can you give it a rest about Laz?"

"No, because even if you're not taking the threats seriously, he would," Prentice said with conviction. "I have no leads on who sent the letters, but Laz has connections on the streets that

I will never have. That man loves you, Journey, and knowing him, he probably would've hunted down the sender by now."

He was right about that. Laz might be mad at her, but he was crazy protective of her. Nothing would change that, not even if their marriage ended. He would still look out for her, and she believed that with all of her heart.

But that was part of the reason why she hadn't told him about any of the threats she'd gotten over the years. He would burn the city down to find whoever was behind them. Then she'd have to visit him in prison for murdering someone.

No, thank you.

Thinking about Laz, Journey remembered that she hadn't turned her phone back on. Since the DA's office was swamped with cases, some of her staff were putting in weekend hours. Unfortunately, they'd been calling her with one question after another for much of the morning. She had shut her phone off when they arrived at the crime scene, intending to turn it back on when they left.

She dug into her oversized bag for the device and wondered if Laz was still giving her the silent treatment.

"No matter what's going on in your marriage, your husband has a right to know that someone is.... *Sonofabitch!*" Prentice slammed on the brake, causing the car to lurch forward.

Journey gasped, banged her hand against the dashboard, and braced herself when the car came to a sudden stop.

"What in the world?" she mumbled.

Her attention was glued to the two huge black SUVs that seemed to come out of nowhere. The menacing-looking vehicles with tinted windows were parked at an angle, effectively blocking them.

Prentice put the car in reverse, glanced back, then cursed. "We're jammed in."

Her head whipped around, and out the back window was another SUV.

Journey swallowed hard as fear charged through her body. Prentice already had his gun out before she reached into her bag for hers. There was a time she didn't carry a weapon, but being married to Laz had changed that. He insisted that she be able to protect herself at all times.

No one climbed out of the vehicles.

"Call 911 just in case this goes sideways," Prentice said, his gun in his hand, resting on his thigh.

Getting a better look at the vehicles in front of them, Journey's eyes widened. She spotted the small decal at the top of the SUV's windshield and gripped Prentice's arm. "I know them."

Those were Supreme Security's vehicles. The decals were only noticeable to someone who knew they were there; they contained computer coding that gave the drivers hands-free entrance into Supreme's parking lot.

As soon as that realization dawned on Journey, Kenton climbed from the passenger side of the first vehicle. He was a mountain of a man, tall, dark, deadly, and built like a defensive tackle. Even from a distance, he was an intimidating force.

Her brother-in-law, Myles Carrington, a former CIA agent turned personal security specialist wasn't as tall and wide as Kenton but looked just as dangerous as he climbed from the driver's side of the SUV. The person in the other truck stayed put.

Glancing over her shoulder at the last SUV, she saw Angelo González, another security specialist, climb out. They were in full defensive mode and had probably found her through the GPS device in the diamond-studded watch that Laz had gifted her when they were first married.

Journey's heart stopped.

Her hands shook.

Dread charged through her body as realization dawned on her.

"Ohmigod. Ohmigod. Ohmigod."

She fumbled with her seatbelt as tears pricked the back of her eyes. "Something's wrong. Something must've happened." Her voice cracked, and she couldn't hide the panic in her words.

"Damn straight, something's wrong. Who the hell are these people?" Prentice roared, tension radiating off of him as he kept his gun lowered but didn't put it away.

"Su—Supreme Security," she managed to say, still fumbling with the damn seat belt. Her hands were shaking too bad to unhook herself.

"Why are they here?"

There was only one reason they would've hunted her down like this, but Journey couldn't form the words. She didn't want to believe anything had happened to her man or her baby. Her heart squeezed, and her chest tightened as she struggled to calm herself.

God, please, please, please. Let them be okay.

Tears blurred her eyes as she watched Kenton's powerful approach. His eyes were covered with dark shades, but the firm set of his mouth let her know that whatever was going on wasn't good. He wasn't dressed in the company's usual uniform of a black suit and tie. No, his attire was casual, and he'd probably been at the party, which only made her more frantic.

She finally managed to unhook her seatbelt and practically fell out of the car when she grabbed the door handle while shoving it open with her shoulder.

"What happened?" she blurted and swayed from the fear pumping through her body. She swiped away a rogue tear. "Where is he? Where's Laz?"

"Grab your stuff and let's go," Kenton said firmly. He might've been the most laid-back and funniest person on Supreme's team, but none of that was present as he held her door.

"Wait. What's happening here?" Prentice asked in a rush.

"Kenton, please." He was such a giant of a man. She had to crane her neck to look up at him. "Just tell me," Journey begged, her voice shaking. "What hap—"

"I'll explain when you get in the truck," he said tightly, not bothering to acknowledge Prentice.

"No! Tell me now, dammit!" she yelled, fear getting the best of her. "Where the hell are my husband and my daughter?"

Kenton went rigid and gritted his teeth. "Laz...he's been shot."

Chapter Six

In a daze, Journey stumbled to the truck with Kenton's large hand at the small of her back. She had to take three steps to his one in order to keep up. Scenarios bombarded her mind, each one worse than the first.

Laz has been shot.

How was that even possible? He'd been at a kid's party.

Journey had so many questions. She wanted to ask about Arielle, but couldn't form the words. Not yet. Not until she was ready for the answer. Because if anything had happened to her baby, it would kill her. As it was, knowing that Laz had been shot made it hard for her to breathe.

They had to be all right. God, please let my family be okay.

By the time they arrived at the truck, she was a nervous wreck. Kenton remained stoic and tight-lipped when he helped her into the back seat of the Suburban. She had to get him to tell her what had happened. She had to know.

"Ke—Kenton," Journey breathed, her body shaking as she struggled to keep herself from falling apart. "Please tell me what's happened. How...." She was trying not to panic and she wasn't a crier, but that didn't stop tears from pushing their way through. She quickly brushed them away. "How is—"

"Buckle up," was all Kenton said before he slammed her door closed and climbed into the front passenger seat.

Her brother-in-law, who was driving, pulled off the moment Kenton got in. The silence was deafening, only making her freak out even more. She needed answers. When neither spoke, dread practically suffocated her.

"Myles...Kenton...*please*. Just tell me he's going to be all right and that my child is okay," she said, unable to hold back the sob that slipped through. "Tell me where they are, please. Where's my family? Are they...."

Kenton jerked around so fast, Journey flinched and slammed back against her seat. A vicious scowl darkened his handsome face.

"Dammit! Why the hell haven't you been answering your phone?" he barked. "The only thing Laz kept saying was 'find my wife. I need my wife!'" Kenton said, his voice rising with every word. "We've been calling you for the past fucking hour! Do you have any idea wh—"

"Hey!" Myles roared as he sped down the highway, weaving in and out of traffic. "Dial it down. Yelling at her ain't gon' help the situation."

Her brother-in-law wasn't a big talker. He was more like the strong silent type, but when he did say something, everyone listened. His grip on the steering wheel and the way his jaw was clenched proved he was just as upset as Kenton. Understandably so since the men of Supreme security were more than just coworkers. They were brothers.

"He needed you. Do you know how we felt when we couldn't find you?" Kenton asked. He wasn't yelling, but the anguish in his tone cut right through Journey. "When Wiz couldn't get a read on your tracker, we didn't know what the hell was going on and whether you'd been attacked, too."

"I'm sorry." She sniffed. "There must've been a dead zone where we were," she said, hating her choice of words seeing that her family could've been killed.

"They might keep Laz overnight," he continued. "He took a round in the shoulder—a clean shot through and through—but he lost a lot of blood. He was in and out of consciousness during the ride to the hospital, but last we heard, he was getting stitched up. Arielle is okay. She's at the hospital with your sister and Dakota."

Journey's chest tightened, and she covered her mouth with her hand. "I'm sorry. God, I'm so sorry." No longer able to hold the tears back as her throat constricted and sobs wracked her body, she cried.

She was sorry that she had bailed on family day. Sorry that she and Laz's last words were angry ones and sorry that this could've been the last time she saw her family.

I should've been there. I should've been with my husband. He needed me.

"Come on, Journey. You're killing me here," Myles said in a consoling tone. "I'm sure Laz is going to be okay. I heard he was giving the hospital staff hell. That's a good sign."

That was a good sign, but it made her ache even more, especially when Myles continued telling her what little he knew about the shooting. Laz had been ambushed, and some man had been killed, but they didn't know too much more than that.

Shock paralyzed her. Laz and Arielle could've been the ones who'd been killed...*and they couldn't find me.*

"We're going to find whoever did this," Kenton said with so much venom in his tone.

Journey was sure that Supreme was already digging for information. They'd probably get answers before the cops.

"Arielle was in the back seat on the floor. She said her daddy said to get on the floor, and she did. She kept saying that she was a good listener," Myles added.

Thank God. Thank God she listened.

But Journey couldn't stop crying. They were only fifteen minutes from the hospital. She had to pull herself together before she got there. She couldn't let her daughter see her crying, especially not after what her baby had been through. But Laz...Laz was never going to forgive her. Her husband had needed her, and she hadn't been there for him.

Journey dug through her handbag for tissues and wiped her face as best she could. Her heart hurt. She was so thankful that Laz was going to be all right, but....

"Give me your watch," Kenton said.

Journey's gaze jerked to his. He was turned in his seat with his hand out.

"No," she said, her breathing coming in short spurts as the meaning of what it meant to give the watch back slapped her in the face. All of the wives who were married to the men of Supreme Security received jewelry with GPS trackers.

If he was asking for it back, that meant that Laz was done with her. That he had given up on her.

She shook her head and folded her arms, covering the watch as if protecting it from Kenton's sight. Childish? Maybe, but she didn't give a damn. She was never giving the watch back.

Most women would've scoffed at the thought of their husbands being able to track them.

Not Journey. After almost dying at the hands of a kidnapper, she welcomed the fact that her husband could find her anytime and anywhere as long as she was wearing the watch. But it meant more than that to her. It was a token of Laz's love.

She never left home without it.

Back then, Laz had promised her that he would never track her unless it was an emergency, and he had exhausted all other ways to reach her. In turn, she had agreed to check in with him either via text or a phone call, especially if she was working late or not coming straight home.

Kenton's expression softened, and he huffed out a breath. "Wiz wants it. He's concerned that we couldn't track you this afternoon, and he's getting it updated with some new tech equipment."

Journey bit her bottom lip, then lowered her gaze. Her heart was breaking. The watch was a symbol of so much more to her. *If she gave it back....* It felt like she was giving up on her marriage or that Laz was giving up on her.

"I can't," she murmured, barely loud enough for them to hear her. "I can't lose him, Kenton."

"Babe, you won't. I know something is going on with you guys, but Laz isn't going anywhere. That I know for a fact," Kenton said with authority.

Journey stared at him through her tears. She wanted more than anything to believe him, but she knew her husband. He wasn't the forgiving type. She was sure that her being unreachable was probably the last straw.

He will never forgive me.

* * *

Minutes later, Myles pulled in front of the emergency room entrance, and Kenton escorted Journey inside. Her heart was beating so fast and hard that it felt like it would leap right out of her chest as they bypassed the emergency waiting room. They took the stairs to a third-floor waiting area, and like Laz, his team hated elevators. They only used them when necessary, claiming it wasn't always safe to be trapped in a floating metal box.

When they arrived on the third floor, Journey willed herself to calm down, to dig deep for the strength she used in court. Her usual breathing technique wasn't working against the anxiousness charging through her body.

At least the tears had stopped. Right now, she considered that a win because the guilt plaguing her was stifling, and she wasn't sure if she'd ever forgive herself for not being available when her family needed her.

"Mase is here somewhere, and he made arrangements for us to use this waiting room for as long as we need," Kenton said, referring to the owner of Supreme Security, Mason Bennett. The man had contacts all over the state and occasionally called in favors. Journey assumed that he had requested a private space until they figured out who was after Laz.

"I'll have to thank him," she said.

When they arrived, the door was closed, and Kenton placed his hand on the doorknob, but he didn't open it. Journey's pulse picked up, thinking he was getting ready to deliver some bad news. She had noticed the small earpieces that he and Myles wore. Had one of the guys given them an update?

"Kenton," she said slowly, bracing herself for the worse.

He removed his shades and stared into her eyes. "Listen, I owe you an apology. I was *way* out of line on the ride here. You didn't deserve the way I spoke to you, and I'm sorry about that. I guess I was just—"

"Worried about Laz," Journey finished. A sliver of relief flowed through her that he wasn't delivering more bad news. "You had every right to be angry. I know how close you and Laz are, and I shouldn't have been MIA. That's...unforgivable."

"Don't be so hard on yourself. Laz knows how important your job is."

"Yeah, but he thinks it's more important than he and Ari, and for a minute there, he might've been right. It's not my intention to put my cases first, but sometimes—"

"Sometimes you can't help it. We all get like that about our jobs, Jay, but you just have to remember that family always comes first. *Always*."

She knew that better than anyone, especially now.

"And for the record, we were worried about you, too. We don't know what we're dealing with yet. This hit could've had something to do with Laz's past, someone gunning for him. Or it could be retaliation for...hell, I don't know...a recent assignment. But we're taking every precaution, and that includes making sure you and Ari are safe. So, when you were unreachable, we feared the worse. Which only freaked Laz out more. He was already being a jerk with the medical staff, but when we couldn't find you, he lost it. They threatened to sedate him."

Journey closed her eyes for a minute and rubbed her forehead as the knife of guilt twisted inside of her. "God, he's going to hate me." She slowly opened her eyes. "I'm so sorry for the trouble I caused, and I promise to never be out of reach again. Does Laz know I'm here?"

Kenton nodded. "When you're ready to go see him, me or one of the other guys will take you to him."

She and her family were close, but their Supreme Security family was just as close. She was so grateful to have all of them in her life, especially at times like this. They all supported each other with the highs and lows that life brought, which made her feel even worse about missing the party earlier.

I have to do better.

"Holler when you're ready," Kenton said, letting her walk into the room while he stayed in the hallway.

It was a simple space with a navy-blue sofa, several multicolored cushioned seats, and a round table with three chairs.

"Oh, thank you, God," Journey choked out when she saw Arielle in Geneva's arms. They were sitting on the sofa near the far corner of the room. Her sister had her eyes closed while she rocked Arielle but glanced up when Journey entered.

"I'm supposed to be the problem child, but you might be catching up with me, sis," Geneva whispered, offering a small smile. "'Bout time they found your ass, er...I mean, butt."

Journey didn't bother responding. She hurried across the cozy room, needing desperately to hold Ari. Geneva tried to stand with Arielle, but being six months pregnant and looking as if she was going to deliver at any moment, her sister remained sitting.

"Thank you for taking care of her," Journey said tearfully as she gathered her child into her arms and held her close. Arielle stirred but didn't wake up. The girl could sleep through a supercell tornado.

"No problem. Dakota was with her for most of the time. She just stepped out to stretch her legs and get a snack."

Journey sat on the sofa next to her, then stared down at Arielle. "How is she? How's my baby?" Journey wanted to wake Arielle, but she seemed so peaceful. Instead, she kissed her cheek and ran her hand over her daughter's head. "I could've lost her," she sobbed. "I don't know what I—"

"She's okay. She's been checked out by a doctor. For the most part, she's fine, except for a bruise on her leg. She's hoarse—I guess from screaming—but other than that, she's her usual bubbly self."

"Thank goodness. I was so scared."

"Have you been to see Laz yet?"

Journey shook her head. How was she going to face him after their argument that morning and what he'd just been through?

Geneva released a long breath and sat back with her hand

covering her rounded belly. "He's mad as hell, Jay. From what we know, he's going to be fine. They were talking about keeping him overnight because of low blood pressure, and his heart rate was really high."

"I gotta go see him. Can you stay with Arielle a little longer?"

"Of course," Geneva said just as Myles walked in, and she smiled at him. "Hey, baby. Thanks for finding my sister."

"No problem," he said, kissing Geneva's lips. "Journey, if you're ready to see Laz, Kenton can take you to his room. Here, I'll take Ari."

Journey wasn't ready to let her daughter go, but she kissed her soft cheek before handing her to him. "Thank you both for everything."

"No thanks necessary. Good luck with Laz," Myles said. "Don't take anything he says too personal."

"Ham said that he was really scared today," Geneva added. "I'm sure my brother-in-law is going to try and take everything that happened today out on you. Stay strong, sis, and be patient with him."

Journey nodded. She loved Laz more than anything, and she prayed he would be all right.

Stay strong.

The words rattled in her mind as she headed to the door. Yeah, she had to be strong because she had no idea what to expect. As long as Laz was okay, they'd figure out how to get their relationship back on track.

At least she hoped.

Chapter Seven

"I need to get the hell out of here," Laz grumbled to Hamilton.

He wanted out of that hospital bed. Not just because he needed to find the bastards who had gunned him down but also because he hated hospitals.

Over a decade on the police force, and he'd only been shot once. Even then, his bulletproof vest had protected him. But this—getting ambushed in broad daylight after years of giving up his badge—was just crazy.

"You're not going anywhere until the doctor says you can leave," Hamilton said as if he had a say in the matter. "Besides, you look like shit."

Laz felt like shit.

His whole body throbbed like one big pulse, and the irritating beeping coming from the machines he was hooked up to made the situation even worse. At least his low blood pressure had risen out of the danger zone, thanks to the IV that was inserted into the back of his hand.

But all of that was overshadowed by thoughts of his wife.

He couldn't explain the fear he'd experienced when no one could find her, not even with the GPS chip in her watch. That's when he freaked out.

The panic of not knowing where Journey was, along with the physical and emotional pain he and Ari had just gone through, had been the perfect storm that had the hospital staff threatening to sedate him. His active imagination had concocted the worst-case scenario—that whoever had come after him had gone after her.

Laz breathed a long sigh and closed his eyes. He'd been relieved to get word that they'd found her with Prentice, but the other part of him was mad as hell. She was never supposed to be out of reach. He would've understood if she'd been in court, but today—a Saturday—there was no excuse he would accept. She was the last person he wanted to talk to or see.

"Journey will be here in a minute," Hamilton said as if reading Laz's mind. "Like you and Ari, Journey's been traumatized enough for one day. Try not to act like a total ass."

Laz glared at him. In light of the shoot-out, if he was honest with himself, he'd admit that he was relieved that Journey hadn't been with him and Arielle earlier. He would've lost his shit if he'd had to worry about her and his daughter getting caught in the crossfire. But there was no way in hell that she was just as traumatized.

"Don't look at me like that." Hamilton's deep voice boomed off the walls as he folded his thick arms across his chest.

At well over six feet tall, he was dressed in a long-sleeved Henley and jeans, looking more relaxed than he usually did at work. At least until he started glaring right back at Laz.

"Just like you freaked out when Journey had been kidnapped back in the day, that's how she was when she learned what happened to you and Arielle. You gotta cut her some slack, man."

"I don't have to do shit," Laz spat, suddenly feeling even more tired than he'd felt moments ago.

Before Hamilton could respond, his cell phone rang. "I mean it, Laz," he said before answering the call.

Whatever, Laz thought. He didn't need another lecture. He appreciated his friend, but no one understood how he felt about Journey not being here when he needed her. Usually, her presence alone calmed him, which was something he could've used hours ago.

Laz stared across the room at the landscape picture hanging against the butter-yellow wall. A sudden bout of sleepiness hit him. He didn't know what he would say to his wife. Anger continued to swirl inside of him, and he feared that if she said the wrong thing to him, he might say something he'd regret.

Now that he knew she was okay, all he wanted to do was close his eyes and pretend the day was just a bad dream.

He wasn't sure if he'd dozed off, but what seemed like minutes later, a sound near the door had his eyes popping open. His gaze landed on the most beautiful woman he'd ever seen in all of his life. His wife.

It didn't matter if he was still pissed; seeing her sexy ass standing inside the door had the heart rate monitor beeping a little faster. Yet, seeing her red-rimmed eyes was like taking a punch to the gut.

Journey wasn't usually a crier, but when she did, it twisted him up inside. He'd vowed to be her protector. Not only did that mean he'd keep her safe, but he had worked his ass off over the years to keep her happy, too.

With his cell pressed to his ear, Hamilton moved to her and kissed her on the cheek before heading to the door. Laz didn't miss the threatening glare his friend shot him on the way out of the room.

"Hey," Journey said.

Laz said nothing.

She moved to the side of the bed, and her sweet, fresh scent teased his nose. All he could do was look at her as the beeping machine sped up. Damn her. Red eyes and all, and even after years of marriage, his stunning, fierce, and intelligent wife still had a visceral effect on him.

At five-six and curvy without being fat, she had a figure that could make a man's mouth water. She was also one of those women who didn't need makeup to enhance her smooth chestnut brown skin, though she wore it anyway. Which only enhanced her beauty.

It was hard to stay mad at her when all he wanted to do was pull her close, kiss her senseless, and never let her go. But thoughts of how she'd been MIA after the incident that could've easily taken his and Arielle's life had fury bubbling beneath the surface.

A knock sounded on the door and jarred him out of his thoughts. A second later, it was pushed open.

"Detectives are here to speak to you," Parker said, glancing at Laz, Journey, and then back to Laz.

Hamilton had told him they'd been there earlier to talk to him, but his friend had held them off. Still, they were the last people Laz wanted to talk to; maybe it was good Journey was there. If he'd learned anything from her, it was never to speak to the cops without a lawyer present.

"Let them in," Journey said before Laz could form any words, and his attention snapped to her. "What? You're going to have to talk to them at some point. Might as well be now—unless you want to tell me what happened first?"

"Nope. Let them in."

Chapter Eight

Journey growled under her breath. He wasn't going to make this easy, but considering how he looked, she couldn't much blame him. Laz wasn't the type of man to complain about being sick or hurt. He was the type to power through, no matter what.

Right now, though, his normally olive skin appeared ashen. He looked sick and drained. His long, dark hair hung loosely around his shoulders, with a few strands sticking out here and there. He was also clearly exhausted. She could see that even with the way he was scowling at her.

That part she could deal with. But seeing him like this—his left arm in a sling and a bruise on the side of his forehead—made her want to crawl into the bed next to him and hold him. She also wanted to beg for his forgiveness. However, the chilly reception he'd given her when she walked in told her she'd be wasting her time.

"How do you feel?" she asked and wanted to kick herself once the words were out of her mouth. It was a dumb question that he didn't bother answering.

Laz continued with the silent treatment as the detectives entered. Journey recognized the older black man, Ted Asher. He'd been a witness on a couple of her cases over the years. "ADA Dimas," he said, giving her a nod and a slight smile. "It's good seeing you again despite the circumstances."

"You too, Detective."

Ted turned to the man who walked in with him. He looked as if he should've been on someone's movie set with his blond hair, blue eyes, and deep tan that made it seem like he'd just returned from the beach. "I'm not sure if you know my partner, Detective Remy Jacobs. He just transferred to our precinct about four months ago. Remy, this is assistant district attorney Journey Dimas, Laz's wife."

"Nice to meet you, ma'am," Remy said and nodded at Laz, who barely spared him a glance.

"How do you feel?" Ted asked him as he and Remy stood on the opposite side of the bed from Journey.

"Like I've been shot," Laz responded dryly.

Journey sighed quietly, still overwhelmed with guilt and the situation. Giving him an *I'm sorry* wasn't going to cut it this time. She knew her husband well enough to know he was probably glad she wasn't with him and Arielle at the time of the shooting. It was the fact that when he sent the guys to find her, they couldn't. That's what had Laz bitter; for that, Journey felt awful.

When she zoned back into the conversation, Laz was telling them why they'd been at the trampoline park.

"I had to park on the street because the parking lot was full, and as I headed to my SUV, a few guys were hanging out nearby. They were doing a...deal. After that, they went their separate ways."

"Do you think they had something to do with the ambush?" Ted asked. "Did you recognize them?"

Laz hesitated for a second before responding. "No."

Silence, except for the machines, filled the space, and Journey wondered if her husband was holding something back. She wouldn't be surprised if he was, because there was no way he was going to trust them completely to find whoever shot at him. Considering the way that the detectives were looking at him as if waiting for him to say more, they suspected he wasn't telling them everything.

"What happened next?" Remy asked.

"Nazir.... Damn." The heart rate machine beeped faster. "I can't believe he's dead. He, um...I met Nazir years ago. He'd been an addict at the time, and...." Laz shook his head, and Journey touched his hand, hoping to offer some comfort. "He saw me, and we stopped to talk. He thanked me for helping him get clean. He hasn't used drugs in over four years."

"Did you and Nazir meet up often?" Ted asked.

"No. I hadn't seen him in years."

For the next few minutes, Journey's heart cracked even more as she was forced to hear what he and Arielle had been through. She would never wish that type of trauma on anyone, and knowing how her husband and child could've died almost brought her to her knees. She was so grateful for Laz's training and how fiercely protective he was. One of many reasons she had fallen in love with him.

She would never forget the first time she and Laz met. Late one night, after work, she was walking to the train station to head home and was attacked. Laz seemed to come out of nowhere and saved her from a vicious mugging. She had gotten hurt, but she honestly felt she would've died that night had Laz not come along when he had.

After that, he continued to watch over her even when she didn't know he was watching. They had become friends. Or at least as friendly as a badass detective who skated on the edge of the law could be with a by-the-book assistant district attorney. From there, after Journey seduced him, they became much more.

Since then, Laz had been her biggest supporter and always had her back. He might've been a little possessive about her and Arielle, but she loved that about him. Their well-being was his top priority. *Always.* His love for her over the years had been unwavering in his words and actions. And even though he was mad at her, Journey knew without a doubt that he would always have her back.

But knowing all of that only made her feel worse.

"Then they just started shooting," Laz was saying when she tuned back in, and Journey's gaze met his. A shiver skittered down her spine. She could see the anger and pain in his eyes. "All I wanted to do was protect my daughter."

"So, you shot back even though people were walking on the sidewalks and driving in their cars," Remy said, a judgmental edge in his tone.

Journey braced herself for what was coming next. Laz never liked people questioning his decisions while he was with Atlanta PD, and that hadn't changed since leaving the force. Especially if he thought he was in the right—which he was most of the time.

She and he had gone head-to-head many times when he was on the police force, and they were working on the same case. Though he used to drive her nuts, their confrontations also strengthened their friendship, leading to a love that she never saw coming.

Laz's hazel-green gaze snapped to the younger detective. "You're damn right I shot back! It was either kill or be killed, motherfucker, and I'd do it again."

Journey ran her hand over his head. "Laz," she warned, hoping he'd settle down but doubting it.

"Don't *Laz* me," he snapped but didn't look at her. "If it had been either of their daughters' lives in danger, they would've done the same thing I did."

"Yeah, but the difference is, we carry a badge!" Remy barked. "You didn't give a damn about anyone else out there on the street. You could've killed an innocent bystander because you were out there shooting recklessly like you own the whole damn...."

Laz bolted upright and lunged at him, immediately silencing the man's words when he grabbed him by the front of his shirt and yanked him forward.

He caught all of them off guard, especially Remy, who lost his balance and fell onto the bed at the same time Laz yelped in pain. The IV had pulled out, and there was blood on the back of his hand, medication dripping from the needle. He dropped back on the bed and started to touch the bandage on his shoulder but stopped himself.

Journey's pulse pounded loudly in her ears. The agony she heard in his groans pierced her in the chest. She was afraid to touch him, unsure if he had other injuries she didn't know about.

"I'm going to go get the nurse," she said in a rush, but Laz weakly grabbed her hand.

"No," he murmured, barely loud enough for her to hear.

His eyes were tightly closed, and his labored breathing had her worried. Her attention went to the white bandage on his shoulder, hoping she didn't see blood and that he hadn't pulled his stitches loose.

Seconds ticked by. No one moved or spoke.

Eventually, Laz released her hand and opened his eyes. The menacing look he gave Remy could've set the man on fire.

Before anyone could speak, a nurse hurried into the room with Parker right behind her. He stayed at the door, looking from one person to the other while the nurse picked up the dangling IV.

"What happened?" she asked and turned off the pump.

"He was being questioned by the detectives…." Journey started to say but stopped and waved her hand, not bothering to finish what she was saying. The heart rate monitor was out of control, and the nurse could quickly tell how the questioning was going.

"Mr. Dimas, I'll have to get someone to reinsert the IV. In the meantime, try to calm down. Do you need me to get you something for the pain? Or maybe the questions can wait." Her gaze went to the detectives.

"Do you guys have any more questions?" Journey asked Ted.

"Yes. A few more," he said.

"Ask them," Laz bit out.

The nurse glanced at Journey before easing back out of the room. Parker slid out, too.

"I heard about you." Remy pointed at Laz, glaring at him with the same disgust Laz was displaying toward him. "I heard that while you were on the job, you did your share of shady shit and was even considered a dirty cop by some. So don't even—"

"Enough!" Journey barked, anger nipping at her nerves. "He was a better cop than you'll *ever* be! Now either ask your questions or get the hell out." She pointed at the door.

"Wow," Remy released a bitter laugh. "So that's how an ADA talks to—"

She jabbed a finger in Remy's direction. "No, that's how I talk to people who verbally attack my husband, detective." Her tone had enough venom to make him take a few steps back. "Ask your damn questions so he can get some rest."

Ted gave his partner a pointed look before turning to Journey. "I'm sorry. Only a few more questions. Laz, did Nazir say anything about anyone being after him? Did he give you any indication that someone was gunning for him?"

"No." Laz shook his head. "He was in good spirits, and we were just talking before all hell broke loose."

"Anyone specifically want you dead?" Remy asked.

"Probably," Laz said without missing a beat as he stared the man down.

"Okay. Let me rephrase the question. Do you know of anyone who would want you dead?"

"Yeah. Probably any of the thousands of criminals I collared while on the job. Pick one, asshole."

Remy threw up his hands. "I think you can take it from here, Ted. I'm out."

Journey watched him leave the room without a backward glance.

Ted leaned closer to Laz. "Your instincts have always been on point. Give me something here, man. Do you think the shooting had something to do with Nazir? Or do you think this was about you?"

Laz shook his head back and forth against the pillow and sighed. "Ted, I wish I knew. I've got nothing. I just need you guys to find whoever did this, and I suggest you find them before I do. Because if I find them first, I can't guarantee anything will be left for you."

"Noted. Take care, my friend. I'll be in touch," the detective said before leaving.

"Have you lost your mind?" Journey ground out, shocked at what he'd said to Ted. "Are you trying to end up in jail?"

Laz didn't speak, only stared at her.

"Oh, so you're giving me the silent treatment. Real mature, Laz. The last time you ended up in jail, I told you that I wouldn't put up with that crap. But if you keep saying stupid stuff like you just did *to a cop*, that's exactly what will happen. There won't be a damn thing I can do to get you off this time. And I won't stick around to try."

He bolted upright, pain twisting his features as fury radiated in his beautiful eyes. They looked lethal enough to kill.

"You have a lot of nerve to stand there and threaten to leave me. You haven't been present in this marriage or this family in months, and don't even get me started about today. You weren't here when I needed you, Journey. When *our daughter* needed you. So back the hell off!"

Damn. Me and my big mouth.

What had she been thinking to bring up his jail time? It had happened shortly before they were married and was part of the reason why he left the police force. It was a long time ago, and Laz wasn't that man anymore.

Yes, he was wrong in threatening to retaliate against the people who shot at him, but she shouldn't have said anything. He'd been through hell today and was emotionally and physically hurt. Her words had just made everything worse.

The door burst open, and Parker and the nurse returned.

"Okay, I don't know what's happening in here, but Mr. Dimas, I'm going to need you to calm down. Your heart rate is—"

"Get my discharge papers," Laz interrupted her. He put his legs over the side of the bed. "I'm out of here."

"Laz, babe, be mad at me all you want, but please don't leave until they—"

Looking past Journey, he made eye contact with the nurse, who stood with her mouth gaping open.

"Get the damn papers," he growled with more force than necessary. "Or I'm leaving without signing them."

The nurse looked at Journey for confirmation, but Journey just shrugged. She thought leaving was a dumb idea, but Laz was the type of man who did whatever he wanted. Consequences be damned.

She feared for his health but also for their relationship. If the last few minutes were any indication, it might be too late for their marriage.

She shook that last thought free.

He could walk out of the hospital—but she would fight like hell before she let him walk away from their marriage.

Chapter Nine

The bumper-to-bumper evening traffic was as thick as usual, and a steady rain pelted the windows while Myles maneuvered through the streets of Atlanta.

So far, the thirty-minute drive was being done in almost complete silence, and Laz appreciated the quietness. No beeping machines, no one asking him fifty million questions, and no one throwing his past indiscretions back in his face.

Laz stiffened when Journey, sitting in the back seat next to him, placed her hand on his thigh without saying anything. He stopped himself from moving away. It was bad enough the way he had snapped at her in the hospital. He wouldn't allow himself to make things worse by jerking his leg away.

He had never loved another human being the way he loved his wife, and that made the tension vibing between them even more frustrating. Something had to give—and soon.

If only he knew how to fix them and their marriage....

"Daddy...." Arielle whined in her sleep, her tiny voice squeezing his heart with so much love. She snuggled closer to him while fisting the front of his shirt but didn't open her eyes.

Laz held her tight to his torso. "Shh, you're okay," he said, gently rocking her and hoping she wasn't having a bad dream. His moves weren't as fluid as usual since he was wearing an arm sling, but Arielle settled back down.

Everyone always talked about how resilient children were. He hoped they were right. He hoped she'd be able to forget what happened and continue being the sweet and lovable kid he knew.

Laz laid his head back and closed his eyes as exhaustion settled deeper into his body. His shoulder throbbed, and he was either going to have to get drunk or break down and take a pain pill to ease some of the agony he was experiencing.

"Do you want me to hold her?" Journey asked quietly.

"No," Laz replied simply and turned his head to look out the dark tinted window.

Usually, he would never allow Arielle to ride in a vehicle without being buckled into her car seat, but he needed to hold her. He needed her close. Every few minutes, he had flashbacks of the shooting. All he could think about was that his child could've been killed. He wasn't really a spiritual man. Yet, he had sent up more than one prayer today for her safety.

Finding those involved in putting him in the hospital would make him feel better and more at ease.

Was there a hit out on him? Possibly. He needed to know who and to learn why. Either way, the motherfuckers were going to wish they had never heard of him. His only concern was how he could take care of it and not land his ass in jail.

The conversation with Journey back at the hospital came to mind. He hated the way he had talked to her, but how dare she throw his stint behind bars in his face. He'd been in the wrong back then, but she seemed to always forget the part of him ending up in that situation because of trying to protect her honor.

Laz straightened in his seat when Myles neared their neighborhood. He had no doubt the former CIA agent was alert and knew they didn't have a tail. However, Laz was a creature of habit. He discreetly glanced around as Myles made a few extra turns while creeping down the quiet streets until he finally pulled into Laz's driveway.

Not even a second later, two other SUVs pulled in front of the house. The extra security might've been overkill, but Laz wasn't taking any chances with his family. He knew Parker and Nelson were in one vehicle, and he assumed Angelo was in the other.

Before Myles could put the car in park, the front door of the house opened, and Journey's parents stepped out. Laz was surprised to see Geneva and Collin, her and Myles's preschooler son, with them.

Myles cursed under his breath at seeing his wife, who was only six months pregnant but looked as if she was going to deliver at any moment, right there on the porch.

Laz almost smiled. He'd been crazy protective when Journey was pregnant with Arielle, but Myles had taken his protectiveness to another level. As a hair salon owner, Geneva was on her feet for much of the day, which was a bone of contention between her and Myles. He had gone as far as hiring extra help for her and had even hired security to follow her around.

Of course, Geneva—being the uncompromising person she was—shot that shit down real quick. She kept the extra salon workers but fired the security personnel.

Myles opened the back door for Journey while Kenton opened Laz's door.

"You need a hand?" Kenton asked as Laz slowly exited the vehicle, carrying Arielle in his good arm.

She might've been a lightweight, but with the pain

charging through his shoulder and arm, it was like he was carrying a two-ton boulder. Instead of saying that, though, he said, "I'm good."

"Well, you look like you're about to keel over. You need to rethink your plans for this evening," Kenton said quietly. "We can start—"

"Not happening. We're sticking with my plan," Laz said just above a whisper, not wanting Journey to hear. "You're taking me to Supreme as soon as I pack a bag."

Kenton sighed loudly and shook his head, probably calling Laz all types of a fool in his mind.

Laz didn't care. As long as he could stay awake, he had every intention of starting his search tonight. Journey would pitch a fit when she found out he planned to stay at Supreme for a few days. Again, he didn't care. As angry as he was at her right now, she was lucky he wasn't moving out of the house for good.

Laz eased up the walkway toward the large two-story colonial they had purchased years ago. He loved this house and had always felt safe, but right now, his nerves were stretched thin. Until he knew whether the shooters had been after him or Nazir, he wouldn't rest.

"I'm so glad you both are okay," Journey's mom said as she placed a kiss on Laz's cheek.

"Thanks, Ivy. Me too. It's good seeing you," he said honestly. His parents had passed away many years ago. Ivy and Logan, Journey's father, were his bonus parents. They lived a couple of hours south of Atlanta and visited often. Having them there made it feel like a typical weekend.

Right now, he needed normal.

Laz stepped onto the porch. Beads of sweat graced his hairline, and his breathing came in short spurts as if he'd run around the block a few times.

"Here, give her to me," Logan said and nodded at Arielle, who was starting to stir.

The big man didn't wait for a response, and Laz gritted his teeth to keep from protesting when Logan took Arielle from him. Usually, he and his father-in-law got along well, but right now, the man was pushing it. Laz wasn't ready to let go of Arielle, and Logan didn't seem to care. The way the old man's eyes analyzed Laz's reaction; it was as if he dared him to say something.

"You need some rest so that you can hunt those bastards down and handle them," Logan said as he walked back into the house with his granddaughter in his arms.

Now *that* was the Logan Laz knew and loved.

Before retiring from Atlanta PD, the old man's reputation wasn't as ruthless as Laz's, but everyone knew that Logan didn't take shit from anyone. For the most part, he had done things by the book, but the man was intimidating as hell. That was saying a lot, coming from Laz. While working for Atlanta PD, Laz had been a *by-any-means-necessary* guy, using his badge to scare criminals into submission.

Logan was different, and it wasn't just his size. There was an arrogant air about him that demanded respect...and maybe even a little fear.

When Laz made it inside the house, his father-in-law still held Arielle, and her eyes popped open. She stretched her neck back to look at Logan.

"Hi, Papa." Her gaze went to Journey's mom, and she squirmed in Logan's arms to sit up. "We—we go to see Minnie Mouse now?" She still sounded sleepy but also hopeful. "Collin!" she screeched when seeing her cousin.

As the four of them headed toward the back of the house where the kitchen and family room were located, Arielle sounded wide awake. Laz heard her start talking about Disney

World while also giving a convoluted version of what occurred earlier. From what Laz could hear, Arielle didn't know she'd been a part of a shooting. She only talked about the loud noises she heard.

Thank God. Hopefully, that was all she remembered.

Still in the large foyer, Laz breathed in a cleansing breath, glad to be home. Before he could head to the stairs that would take him up to the bedroom, Geneva strolled over. She slid her arm through his and laid her head on his good shoulder.

"I'm glad you're going to be okay. Especially since I'm sure you want to go after the assholes who put a bullet in you. Let me know if you want backup. I'm right there with you if needed."

Laz couldn't help but chuckle. He didn't have any sisters, only a brother, but if he had one, he'd want her to be just like Geneva. According to Journey, her sister was his female equivalent, and he could definitely see the similarities in their personalities.

Though Journey had plenty of sass and didn't let anyone walk over her, Gen took being a badass to another level. Whoever came up with the term "ride or die" was talking about his sister-in-law. She was fearless, loyal, and always ready to throw down. Marriage hadn't changed that. Like some of the men Laz knew, Geneva was a fight-first-and-ask-questions-later type person. The woman was scary as hell, and she was probably serious about having his back, despite being hugely pregnant.

"Thanks, Gen." He kissed her forehead before she lifted her head from his shoulder. "You'll be the first person I call if I need help. But just a heads-up. Your husband is on his way over here, and he doesn't look happy."

"Aww, hell. Let me go and smooth things over. I was

supposed to be at home like a good little wife," she said as she strolled away.

Laz had just started up the stairs when Journey came from the living room area. Just as she reached him, Kenton and Angelo strolled into the house.

"Guys, thanks so much for everything you've done for us today," Journey said. "I know you're probably tired and ready to head home. We can take it from here."

"They're not going anywhere," Laz said, with more bite behind his words than intended. This was why he had to get the hell out of there before he made the tension between him and Journey even worse. "You're going to have a security detail until further notice. At least two guys at all times."

"Laz," she started, and that one word held a ton of frustration.

"This is not up for negotiation." He didn't care how mad she made him at times. Her safety was at the top of his list of priorities, and until he knew who or what they were dealing with, he wanted her protected. "I especially want someone around since I won't be here."

Journey's perfectly arched brows scrunched together, and she jammed her hands onto her hips. "What are you talking about?"

"I'll stay in one of the crash rooms at work for a few days."

When his boss Mason Bennett had purchased an old warehouse to house Supreme Security, he had converted it into a state-of-the-art facility. In addition to tech-smart meeting rooms, a cook's kitchen, a gym, and a weight room, he'd had the foresight to include several rooms similar to studio apartments. Some of the security specialists, especially those who lived outside of Atlanta, used the spaces to grab a nap in between assignments instead of going home.

"Whenever you're at work or too busy for our daughter

during that time," Laz continued, knowing he was being an ass, "one of the guys will bring Arielle to me."

"First of all, how are you making these decisions without discussing them with me? Secondly, Arielle is going to Florida with my parents as planned."

"Like hell she is," he roared. "Plans have changed."

Journey moved closer to him, and her *I'm-not-taking-your-shit-tonight* demeanor was fully in place. He loved this woman like crazy, and she was sexy as hell when she was angry. Any other time, he could appreciate the can of verbal whoop-ass she was about to unleash, but he wasn't in the mood.

"I know you've been through hell today," she said with controlled fury, "but what you're not going to do is come in here and start telling me how things are going to be."

From his peripheral, Laz saw the moment when Kenton and Angelo eased into the living room, which was probably for the best. He had a feeling this argument was going to blow up at any minute.

"I'm done talking to you." Laz started up the stairs to their bedroom.

"Good, then you can do the listening," Journey said, stomping up the stairs and shoving past him. "I'll meet you in the bedroom."

A smart man would do a one-eighty and head back down the stairs, but Laz never claimed to be smart. He wasn't in the mood for a drag-down blowout with Journey, but it was safe to say that's exactly what was about to happen.

"You want an update before you go and face the firing squad?" Parker asked from behind him.

Laz turned to his friend, who was leaning his shoulder against the wall near the bottom step as if he didn't have a care in the world.

Parker had moved to Atlanta from Chicago, hired by

Supreme, and was assigned to the *Atlanta's Finest* team a couple of years ago. The former SWAT officer fit in perfectly. He was one of the youngest ones in the group, a weapons specialist, and essentially fearless. The man had nerves of steel, and Laz loved having him on the team.

"You got something and didn't tell me?" Laz asked as he walked back down the few steps he'd taken. "Tell me you found the bastards."

"Haven't found them yet, and I'm not sure what Ham has already filled you in on. So, some of this might be a repeat," Parker said.

Laz hadn't been in a good head space, so he didn't know much about what happened after he was rushed to the hospital. Yes, he'd wanted to know who the hell had shot at him, but earlier, he hadn't been ready to hear anything. His number-one focus had been on finding Journey.

"Angelo chased after the car on foot. He wasn't able to get close enough to get the license plate number, but he did get a partial plate off the car,"

"Did he tell Ted?" Laz asked.

Parker shook his head. "Nope. He knew you'd want to stay ahead of the cops on this."

There was nothing more special than having people in your life who knew you well. This situation was going to be tricky, especially since Nazir had been killed. The cops would be all over the case, trying to piece the events together and find Nazir's killer.

Laz didn't want anyone getting in trouble for withholding evidence, but the men of Supreme Security knew what to hold back and what to share with the detectives.

"Wiz is doing a search based on the make and model of the car, as well as the partial plate. Last I heard, he'd found over three hundred possibilities, but he assured Ham that he'll narrow the list down."

Laz nodded. Cameron "Wiz" Miller was one of the owners of Supreme Security-Chicago and their go-to person for all things technology. The man was a computer guru and a hacker extraordinaire. What he could do with technology was mind-blowing, and he was constantly developing something new that could help them with their jobs—such as GPS devices for the women in their lives. All of the wives had a piece of jewelry that held a GPS chip.

Which reminds me....

"Do you guys have Journey's watch?"

"Yeah, Kenton got it from her, but not without a fight." Parker laughed. "When he asked for it, she refused to give it to him."

Laz frowned. "Why?"

"Well, it happened after they found her, and he read her the riot act for not having her phone on. Anyway, she wasn't giving it up at first. It wasn't until he assured her that Wiz just wanted to update the GPS device that she finally handed it over."

Damn. "That's on me," Laz said.

Journey thought he no longer wanted her protected: that he didn't care—which wasn't the case at all. If anything, he wanted double security on her, at least until they knew who or what they were dealing with.

"One more thing," Parker said, all humor erased from his face as he pushed away from the wall.

Laz braced himself for whatever was coming next. "What?"

"Ashton dug into Nazir's background, talked to his employer, and stopped by his apartment that he shared with a roommate. Everyone had only good things to say about him.

We were going to keep digging to ensure we ruled him out as the target, but...."

"But?" Laz prompted, anxiousness slowly building inside his body as he waited for Parker to continue.

His friend stared him in the eyes, and his jaw was clenched tight enough to crack his teeth. "We just got word that there was a tracker under the back bumper of your truck. You were the target, Laz."

Chapter Ten

Journey stormed into their bedroom and wanted to slam the door in Laz's face, but she refrained. Her husband had done plenty of crap to anger her over the years, but today, the way he'd been treating her was unacceptable.

She paced the length of their bedroom twice to calm herself. It wasn't working. Not even the soft lighting from the bedside table lamps and the tranquil blue-gray walls could soothe her tattered nerves. By the time Laz walked in, she had hoped to have quieted the angry thoughts running through her mind.

Instead, she wanted to knock some sense into her husband.

But when she swung around to face him, some of her anger drifted out of her like air from a balloon. Her big, strong man was hunched forward slightly and clearly in pain. His long, dark hair was pulled back into a ponytail at the nape of his neck, giving her a clear view of his pale face and pinched features.

Without a word, he shuffled past her and sat in an overstuffed chair near the windows. The blinds were drawn, and he didn't bother turning on the lamp perched on the small table between the chairs. It was semi-dark in that corner, but there was just enough light in the room for her to see him watching her.

"I hate this," she mumbled, unsure what part she hated the most. The fact that they were fighting or the fact that he wasn't himself tonight.

She wanted so badly to sit in his lap and wrap her arms around him—something she did often, but she couldn't. Unless she wanted her ass to end up on the carpeted floor because she had a feeling that that was where he'd dump her if she tried to snuggle up to him. He might be in serious pain, but the way he was glaring at her with his beautiful hazel-green eyes told her he was ready for a fight.

"I'm sorry, all right?" Journey said. "God knows I wish I was there to...."

"No." Laz shook his head. "I'm glad you weren't at the scene. I have never been as afraid as I was, knowing there was a chance that Arielle could've been hit by a bullet. I can't even explain that type of fear, but it would've *killed me* had you been there and in danger. I wouldn't have been able to handle it."

Her heart flipped inside of her chest. She had no doubt that he would've done the same thing he did—fight to get to her and make sure she was safe. With him sharing that information with so much emotion in his tone, she knew their love for each other was stronger than any disagreement they could ever have.

Yet, the tension between them was proof that it took more than love to keep a marriage together.

"Laz—"

"I just wanted you to be there when I needed you the most —*after* everything went down. Arielle was inconsolable, and hearing the fear in her cries...." His words trailed off, and

Journey thought he was done talking, but then he said, "I needed you."

His voice cracked, and he rubbed his hand over his mouth and down his beard. He laid his head back and closed his eyes.

The guilt Journey had experienced earlier was back with a vengeance, stabbing her in the chest.

"You're my everything, which is why this shit we're going through is hard as hell," Laz bit out, emotion clogging his throat.

"I messed up," Journey admitted and dropped down in the opposite chair. "I put the job first when I promised you that I'd take today off. I'm sorry. I am so sorry you guys couldn't find me."

She didn't bother explaining how important her case was or how their key witness was dead, while some of the other witnesses were running scared. At the moment, none of that mattered, and Laz had heard it all before with different cases, which made her feel even worse.

"I love you more than anything in this world," she said, not bothered by the fact that his eyes were still closed. "I know lately it doesn't seem like it, but it's true. Thing is, though, I'll be damned if I let you talk to me any kind of way like you did today."

He opened his eyes, but kept his head back and stared at the ceiling. When he didn't speak, Journey stood and started pacing again. This time she shortened the distance and paced back and forth in front of the chairs.

"Now, let's discuss what you said downstairs," she continued. "I'm a grown woman, Laz. You might be my husband, and normally, I go along with what you say."

He made a sound that resembled a grunt but didn't say anything more.

Journey fought a smile. "Okay, maybe I don't go along with

anything without pushback, but I trust your judgment more than anyone's in this world. That said, though, I can't do my job with security following me around."

"It's non-negotiable, Jay," he said just above a whisper, exhaustion dripping from every word. It was a good sign that he was calling her by the nickname he'd given her. "I need to know that you're protected while the guys and I figure out what the hell is going on."

Journey listened and knew she would be wasting her time arguing this subject. Besides, she didn't want him worrying about her while trying to figure out who had ambushed him earlier. "Fine, but the guys have to do what I say and not scare my witnesses away."

Silence.

She'd take that as a win.

"Secondly, I understand why you want to keep Arielle close. If I could, I'd hold her and never let her go, but she'll be safe with my dad in Florida. If we have to, we can hire security to go with them. Either way, I think she should go. Also, Gen said that she and Myles are letting Collin go with them. We have to let Arielle go on this trip."

More silence.

"Besides, if we're going to find these people who came after you, wouldn't it be better if our daughter was someplace safe?" She needed him to know that she was in complete support of him hunting these assholes down. "*We* won't be able to do that if we're worrying about and shuffling Arielle around this week."

Laz lifted his head slightly, and his gaze finally met hers and held. Her heart turned over in her chest as she stared into his eyes that were no longer shooting daggers at her.

"What do you mean, *we*?" he asked. "I don't want you anywhere near this situation."

"Well, since I already know that you're not going to let the cops handle this case, I'm going to do whatever I can to help you. Just let me know if the DA's office can be of assistance... legally, that is."

He didn't respond.

It was a shame she had to add that last part, but with her husband, it was necessary. His intentions were always good, but Laz could be a loose cannon at times when he was determined to set something right.

"Also, you're going to break Arielle's heart if she can't go to Disney World. Lastly, I don't want you staying at Supreme and leaving me here by myself."

"You won't be by yourself."

"You know what I mean. How will it look you sleeping at Supreme and me here?"

"Journey, I don't give a damn how it looks. I need space."

"From me," she said more as a statement than a question. "Leaving me is not going to fix anything."

Silence...again.

She blew out a frustrated breath. "Well, at least stay here tonight. You need some rest before you get to work."

A soft, familiar knock sounded on their bedroom door.

"Mommy." Arielle's sweet little voice floated through the door before she knocked again.

After getting caught naked one too many times by their daughter, who insisted on walking into their room at the most inopportune times, they'd had to set some rules. She wasn't allowed to step into the room, even if the door was open, without asking permission. It had taken time, patience, and a few tears—not just Arielle's—for her to finally learn.

"Mommy, Daddy, I want to come in."

"Come in, baby," Journey said.

Arielle ran in and wrapped her arms around Journey's legs, almost knocking her over.

Journey picked her up and placed kisses all over her face. "Hey, my sweet girl. How are you?"

"Good. Me and Collin going to Disney World!" Her bright eyes, so much like Laz's, were sparkling with excitement. Then she saw her father sitting across the room. "Daddy!" She squealed. "Down, Mommy. I—I want...get down."

Journey set her on her feet, and Arielle took off across the room but stopped short before reaching Laz.

"Daddy hurt?" she asked in a small voice and seemed scared to move forward.

"Come here, sweetie," Laz said sleepily and stretched out his arm to her.

Arielle went but kept her gaze on the sling that his other arm was in.

Laz slowly lifted her onto his lap and kissed her. "Where you been?"

"Grandma gave me and Collin chicken nuggets."

"Were they good?" he asked.

Her head bobbed up and down. "Papa taking me to see Prin—Princess Tiana. I'm going to have fun!"

Journey was worried about their child's mental health and how the shooting might've affected her. At the moment, Arielle seemed like her usual animated self.

"I'm going to see Minnie Mouse, too!"

Journey fought the smile itching to break free at the defeated look Laz threw at her over Arielle's shoulder.

The big softy. There was no way he could say no to their daughter.

"I guess we should go and pack your suitcase, huh?" Journey said.

"Ari?" Collin called from the hall before showing up in the doorway. "What you doing?"

Journey smiled. He was a cutie and the spitting image of

Myles. His hair was cut low, and he had smooth, tawny-brown skin and chubby cheeks, even though he was thin. And then there were those onyx eyes that held the same intensity as his father's. Journey found it hilarious that he also had Myles's cool and calm demeanor, even at a young age.

Arielle scooted off of Laz's lap and ran to the door. "Hurry, Mommy. We gotta go to Disney World!"

"I'll be right there," Journey said and glanced at Laz. "Can she go?"

He released a long sigh and stood. "Yeah, but not without a security detail."

Journey smirked. "Good luck in telling my dad that." She might've tossed the idea out there, but she didn't know Laz would go for it. "He's not going to take too kindly of you thinking he's too old to take care of his grandkids."

"Yeah, whatever," Laz mumbled.

"Why don't you try and get some rest?"

He was already heading to the bed before Journey could get all the words out of her mouth, and she grabbed a pair of pajama bottoms from his drawer and took them to him.

"Do you need help with your shirt?" He was wearing a black button-down that Mason had brought to the hospital. "And it might be time to change your bandage," she said, starting toward the bathroom for supplies.

"Not right now," he said, stopping her. "I just...I just need a little sleep."

Without removing the sling from his arm, he gingerly laid back against the mattress and closed his eyes. Within seconds, he was snoring.

Journey stood there with her heart full and just watched him. For the umpteenth time that day, she thought about how she could've lost him and Arielle.

He'd said that it would've killed him if anything had

happened to her, and she knew that type of fear. She couldn't imagine her life without him. It didn't matter if he was as stubborn as a mule or if he was often difficult to deal with. She loved him.

As she walked out the door, Journey realized she had won a couple of battles in the last few minutes. Yet, the hardest one—convincing him not to give up on them—wasn't going to be as easy.

Her marriage was still in danger, and an *I'm sorry* wasn't going to fix it.

Chapter Eleven

Laz pulled his wool cap lower over his eyes as the chilled air whipped around him. He burrowed deeper into his leather jacket despite the awkwardness of having one arm through the sleeve and the other in a sling under the coat.

At least he was warm, but five o'clock in the morning was too damn early to be moving around the city before having at least two cups of coffee. Even so, that didn't stop him, Parker, and Ashton from skulking through a dark alley. They skirted around potholes, cans, bottles, and trash, trying to avoid waking up the neighbors.

When Ashton called an hour ago with news the car had been found, Laz had just dozed back to sleep after seeing his in-laws and Arielle off. His father-in-law decided they'd leave in the middle of the night to get a head start on traffic. It was hard to let Arielle go, but Journey had been right. Their daughter would be safe, and he wouldn't have to worry about her while hunting down the people who tried to kill him.

"Shit!" Startled, Laz pulled up short when a stray cat

leaped from behind a dented trash can and darted across the alley in front of them.

"Just a cat," Parker said, speaking the obvious before they continued forward.

Limited lighting guided their way as they traipsed toward the middle of the alley past a few run-down houses and a couple of vacant lots where houses used to stand. The bulbs in most of the streetlamps were blown or shot out, and only one or two garages had motion lights. It was a good thing Parker and Ashton had thought to bring flashlights.

Laz was definitely off his game. Half asleep and in physical pain, while he got dressed, the only thing he'd grabbed before being whisked away by Parker was ID, house keys, and his gun. He had discreetly thrown some clothes in a duffel bag when he'd gotten up to see Arielle off, and he remembered to grab it before leaving the house.

Sleeping at Supreme for a few days would be for the best, but he was sure Journey wouldn't be happy when she found out he had left. They needed space, and he couldn't handle any more arguments, not right now. Not when all his focus needed to be on finding those who wanted him dead. Once that was done, he'd figure out what to do about his marriage.

"There it is." Ashton pointed to a black sedan a few yards away.

As he suspected, the car had been reported stolen the night before the shooting. If Ashton had gotten a tip about the vehicle's location, that meant the cops would find it soon if they didn't already know about it. He and the fellas had to do a quick search before they lost their opportunity, and even though there was a possibility they wouldn't find anything, he had to try.

"Well, Laz, it looks like during the shoot-out you indeed made contact," Parker said, his small flashlight illuminating the passenger side of the vehicle where there were several bullet holes.

"Good, now tell me there's a dead body or two inside with one of my bullets lodged right between their eyes," Laz grumbled and peeked into the vehicle, made easy by three of the windows being rolled down. "It looks like there's blood on the inside of the door."

That was a good sign as far as he was concerned. Unfortunately, there wasn't much, meaning he might've wounded one of the guys, but it probably wasn't a life-threatening injury.

When Laz moved to the back window, he realized Ashton was several feet away. His pinched features sent a wave of unease clawing through Laz.

"What is it? What's wrong?"

Ashton gave his head a slow shake. "Sorry, I had a moment. The last time I searched a car...." His words trailed off, and Laz and Parker looked at each other, recalling that night over a year ago.

Damn. Laz just remembered what he'd said a moment ago about hoping they'd find a couple of dead bodies, and he wanted to kick his own ass.

Ashton was remembering the night a dead body—someone he knew—had been found in the trunk.

"Hey, man," Parker said. "You can hang back. Laz and I can handle this. Well, I can, at least. Not sure how much good Laz will be with one arm and grimacing every few minutes."

"Whatever, man," Laz said. "But Ash, he's right. We got this."

"Nah, I'm good." Ashton approached the car. "We need to do this quick so that you can let Ted know that the vehicle has been found," he said, referring to the detective on the case, a man they'd both worked with and respected.

For the next few minutes, with gloved hands, they all took a section of the vehicle to search. Laz moved around to the driver's side since he could only use his right hand. He checked the pocket in the door, under the seat, and between the seat and the center console.

Nothing.

At least nothing worth mentioning like a grocery list, a faded store receipt, and cookie crumbs.

The others made quick work of checking the glove box, center console, between and under the front seats as well as the back. They found no clues to lead them to the people who had stolen the vehicle.

Laz had just closed the back door on the driver's side of the sedan when an SUV with police lights flashing pulled into the alley.

Dammit.

After he and the guys finished searching the vehicle, he had planned to contact Ted. Looked like that wouldn't be necessary since the detective stepped out of the truck on the passenger side. He definitely wasn't happy to see them.

"What the hell?" Ted snapped, looking mainly between Laz and Ashton. "You guys, of all people, know better. I should arrest you for interfering with an active investigation."

Laz released a ragged sigh. It was too damn early for any of this. "I planned to call you," he said. *When we were done*, he wanted to add but didn't.

"But you didn't," Remy said, anger marring his tanned skin as his steady gaze stayed on Laz.

It didn't take a genius to know the man didn't like him, which was fine. The feelings were mutual. The guy was too pretty, too uptight, and if Laz's suspicions were correct—too soft. Remy was the type of guy who was all talk and couldn't back up what he was spewing. A guy who probably followed the rules a hundred percent and ignored the gray areas—and in law enforcement work, there were always gray areas.

"How'd you know the car was here?" Ashton asked Ted.

"A few hours ago, a neighbor reported an abandoned car with bullet holes sitting out here. When the 911 operator entered the info into the system, including the license plate number, we were alerted. Now imagine my surprise to find you guys here. I won't even bother asking how you found the vehicle."

Ted was old-school police. He supported the men and women in blue to the core. Since Laz and Ashton were former Atlanta PD, the older man trusted that they wouldn't sabotage his case. He would also give them grace in knowing how important it was that Laz found the people who gunned him down.

"We could arrest all of you for tampering with physical evidence. A felony," Remy said, his gaze steady on Laz.

Now, this motherfucker was a different story, Laz thought.

The man's holier-than-thou attitude was on full display, and there was no doubt he had it in for him. Laz wasn't sure if it was because of his past reputation while with Atlanta PD, or it could be jealousy, for all Laz knew. Whatever it was, he wasn't going to let this cocky young punk get under his skin.

He glared right back at the man.

"But we won't," Ted added quickly, picking up on the tension. "Just tell me that you didn't touch, find or take anything."

"We didn't," Ashton said before Laz could respond. "We just got here."

"Well, did you find anything?" Ted asked as he slipped on a pair of latex gloves.

"Nope." Laz moved to stand near the front passenger side. "Except there's blood on the inside of this door. Looks like I might've clipped one of the perps, but not enough to cause real damage."

Remy stood a few feet away, shaking his head. "Shooting in the middle of a busy street and possibly wounding someone. We should have you down at the station being questioned and maybe even charged."

"Man, quit being such an asshole," Laz said before he could stop himself.

The guy was itching for a fight—one that Laz had no intentions of starting. Whether he and Journey were on good terms or not, what she thought still mattered to him. She had already reamed him out at the hospital about what he'd said to Ted. He wouldn't make that mistake again. Besides, if things went sideways with the case, he didn't want to put Ted in a compromising position.

As for Remy? The guy could tumble off a side of a cliff, and Laz wouldn't stop his fall.

Remy stomped closer. "*You?* You're calling someone an asshole? Man, from what I hear—"

"I don't give a damn what you've heard about me or who you've heard it from. If it'll make you feel more like a man to haul my ass downtown, fine. Let's do this. Just let me call my lawyer, and we can make a move.

Remy snorted. "Your *lawyer*?" He mumbled something else under his breath about the ADA as he moved back to where he was initially standing, and Laz slowly turned to face him fully.

"What did you say?"

At first, he thought the guy wasn't going to repeat himself, but then he spoke. "I said I don't know what the ADA sees in you. She could've done a lot better, but she chose to marry a thug."

Someone groaned. Laz wasn't sure if it was Ashton or Parker, but he felt them both inch a little closer to him.

Laz eyed Remy up and down, then he laughed. "So, what I'm hearing is that you think you'd be better suited for her."

"Well, I wasn't thinking that, but yeah, I do."

Laz burst out laughing. "Man, my lady is *way* too much woman for you. You couldn't handle her even on your best day. I suggest you quit fantasizing about *my wife*."

The man's blue-eyed gaze darkened, and a vein in his forehead popped out. It looked as if Remy wanted to say more but kept his mouth shut.

Laz moved away from the vehicle and approached him but managed to stop an arm's length away. He didn't trust himself to get any closer. "And if your dumb ass even thinks about stepping to her, it won't end well for you."

Remy's blond eyebrows pulled into a perfect V. "Are you threatening me?" Remy moved close enough for Laz to smell cinnamon on his breath.

"No."

"No, he wasn't," Ashton and Parker said at the same time.

So focused on Remy, Laz hadn't realized that they had moved closer, along with Ted, and were crowding them.

"I wasn't threatening you. Just stating a fact." Laz didn't bother explaining what he'd do to him if he ever got word that he made a pass at Journey.

Instead, he said suggestively, "She's got a wicked mouth and tongue." An eerie calmness settled over him. "If you approach her the wrong way, she'll definitely put you in your place. I'm not threatening you, but I suggest you tread lightly with my wife. Don't take her beautiful face and slammin' body for weakness. She's a *beast* and will send you away with your tail between your legs."

"Well, we'll see." Remy grinned.

"Okay, that's enough," Ted spat as Laz, with his fist balled and seeing red, took a step forward simultaneously.

Ashton, like a snake in the grass, moved quickly. He grabbed Laz's good shoulder and turned him with force. Parker was behind Laz and nudged his back, both men effectively moving him away from Remy.

"We'll catch you later, Ted," Ashton said over his shoulder as they guided Laz the way they came. "Remy...it's been real."

"You should've let me punch the guy because I have a feeling before this is all said and done, it's going to happen."

"Not if we can help it," Ashton said.

"You can let me go now," Laz ground out and shook out of Ashton's hold.

The moment they backed off, Laz removed his gloves and dug into his jacket pocket for the burner phone that Myles had slipped to him the night before.

"Who are you calling?" Parker asked as they walked up the alley back the way they came.

"Someone I should've called yesterday."

Laz dialed a number he knew by heart. As the phone rang, he pulled a single cigarette and lighter from the inside pocket of his leather jacket and lit it. He had promised Journey that he would quit, and he had. Well, at least for the most part. It was only when he was stressed that he lit up.

He took a long drag from his cigarette, then tilted his head back and slowly released smoke into the cool air. A second puff, and he could already feel the tension rolling off of him.

The person finally answered, growling into the phone. "Who the hell is this? Do you know what fucking time it is?"

"C-Dogg, it's Laz. I need your help."

Chapter Twelve

"Thanks for getting some of the girls together. I really needed a change of pace tonight," Journey said to Egypt, who sat in the back seat of the SUV with her.

Typically, the wives of Supreme Security met up once a month on a Saturday for dinner and drinks, usually at one of their homes. With the emotional turmoil Journey was experiencing, she couldn't wait for the next meetup. It wasn't scheduled for another couple of weeks, but she needed some bonding and conversation now.

"Not a problem. I'm glad you called," Egypt said, squeezing Journey's hand. "It's nice to get out, and it gave Junior a chance to hang out with his Uncle Nelson."

Journey smiled. She couldn't imagine big, tough Nelson being on babysitting duty. Especially looking after an active one-year-old.

Nelson wasn't related to Egypt, although, for years, they led everyone to believe that they were brother and sister. Actually, Nelson was her handler when she was in WITSEC many years ago. Egypt had been assigned a few handlers through the years, but she and Nelson had kept in touch, even when he left the US Marshals.

Journey leaned over and whispered in Egypt's ear, "Thanks for talking your husband into letting us all get together."

Originally, Kenton had shot down the idea, claiming that the guys were already spread thin. He also hadn't thought it a good idea for Journey to be around the other women in case she really was in danger.

Journey wasn't sure what Egypt had said to her husband to get him to change his mind, but she would be forever grateful. If she had to go home to that empty house, she would've driven herself nuts.

"Be sure to thank Dani, too," Egypt whispered back, and Journey agreed.

Dani, Ashton's wife, owned the Double Trouble bar with her brother and had come through big-time. Journey had suggested that the wives meet at her and Laz's house. She figured that made the most sense since security was already stationed there.

That was another idea Kenton hadn't liked. He didn't come around until Dani offered up the bar for them to use.

The wives were proving to be just as resourceful as their men, and Journey had to think of a way to thank them for coming through for her.

A short while later, Kenton pulled in front of the bar. He and Angelo climbed out of the front seat at the same time. Their moves were perfectly in sync. Journey wasn't sure if that was training or just instinct. Either way, it was no wonder that Supreme was one of the most elite security firms in the country.

After glancing around and checking their surroundings, the guys opened the back doors.

"You two already know the drill. Don't even think about

leaving here without us or going outside for any reason," Kenton said as he escorted them to the bar's main entrance while Angelo stayed with the truck.

The year before, when Dani had almost been kidnapped, Ashton had insisted on around-the-clock security, especially when she was working. Now there were always two security specialists on duty who blended in with the crowd.

"Jay, if anything feels off or if anyone approaches you who you don't know, signal for one of the guys or text me," Kenton continued. "Until we figure out this situation with Laz, we don't want to take any chances, all right?"

"Okay," she said, accepting the one-armed hug he gave her before he pulled Egypt to his side.

Journey didn't stick around to watch the two play kissy-face. She might've been thrilled that her friends found each other and fell in love, but when her own marriage was on shaky ground, seeing happy couples hugged up to each other triggered her insecurities. For a person who once had never planned to get married, she couldn't imagine her life without Laz. She wasn't sure what she'd do if he left her for good.

Realizing her thoughts were veering into depressing territory, she lifted her head and pulled her shoulders back. Tonight was about having a good time with her girls.

Journey strolled into the building, and the high energy coaxed her further inside. She held her purse close to her side and squeezed by a small group of people standing around one of the tall tables. As she weaved around others, she noted how busy the bar was for a Sunday evening. It probably had to do with several basketball games and other sports playing on the wall-mounted televisions hung all over the large space.

Double Trouble wasn't just some hole-in-the-wall bar. There was plenty to do for someone who just wanted to get out of the house and hang with friends. The small stage and a dance floor at the back of the building were well used when there was live entertainment. Pool tables and dartboards were stationed in the far-left corner of the building. When the weather was nice, people often sat outside on the large patio deck that offered a great view of the city of Atlanta.

Journey was nearing the last booth when she saw a familiar face. *Tony Price*, her ex. His surprised gaze met hers, and his smile was warm and inviting, like usual. They had parted on good terms...sort of. After dating for years, Tony wanted marriage. More specifically, he wanted to marry her.

She told him repeatedly that she had no intentions of getting married—*ever*. At the time, her career was everything to her, and she couldn't see herself tied down. That didn't mean she hadn't loved Tony, but she hadn't loved him enough for that type of commitment.

Never say never, her sister Geneva had once told her. That was shortly before Journey started dating Laz and, within months, married him.

It was then that she realized that she might've loved Tony, but it wasn't an *I-can't-live-without-you* type of love. Nothing like what she felt for Laz. There were times when her deep love for her husband scared her to death. She never knew she could love someone as completely as she did him.

Needless to say, the first time that she and Tony ran into each other after she was married had been uncomfortable. He reminded her then that she'd told him that she didn't want marriage, that she wasn't the marrying type. In the end, though, he wished her and Laz well.

That had been several years ago, and since then, they'd been friendly whenever they saw each other.

As he stood from the booth, Journey took in his appearance. Though there were some differences, he was still a nice-looking man with skin the color of mocha and friendly dark eyes. When they dated, he was always well-groomed, wore his hair closely cropped, and was a conservative dresser.

Now, at almost six feet tall, his previously slim runner's build was replaced with a man who clearly lifted weights. He wasn't super muscular, but the lightweight blue sweater he was wearing molded over his well-defined upper body and emphasized his broad shoulders. His hair was a little longer. Not quite an afro, but getting there, and the mustache and beard was neat but longer than she would've ever imagined he'd wear it.

"Well, if it isn't the most beautiful ADA in the world," he said by way of greeting, and hugged her.

"I see you're still a sweet talker," she said, grinning.

"I'm speaking the truth." He leaned back slightly, and his gaze traveled the length of her. "You look amazing."

"Thank you."

If her skin was lighter, he'd be able to see her blushing. Now that she ran into him, Journey was glad she had opted to wear the red off-the-shoulder sweater dress that molded over her curves and her tall, knee-high black boots that demanded attention. All week, she dressed professionally in her designer suits, but her weekend attire gave her a chance to express her fun, carefree side.

"This is a pleasant surprise. When did you start hanging out at bars?" Tony asked, still eyeing her with interest.

"Actually, I don't hang out often, but I'm meeting some friends here." Not wanting to talk about herself, for fear he'd ask how her marriage was, she redirected the conversation. "How have you been? How's business?"

They talked for a few minutes, and she listened as he told her how he was expanding his computer repair business. Journey was glad that he was doing well.

"So, are you seeing anyone?" she asked.

He had told her a lot about what was going on in his work

life, but she was curious about his personal life. He had always wanted to get married, and she figured that, after they broke up, he would've found someone to settle down with.

His left brow lifted, and a crooked grin spread across his handsome face. "Why? Are you interested? Because if you're—"

"I'm not," she said quickly with a laugh. "I was just curious. That's all."

He laughed with her. "I'm messing with you. I know Laz would never let you go."

He and Laz had met and were cordial, especially since they were both active with *Save Our Boys*, a nonprofit organization.

Tony had been on the board of directors for years. The nonprofit focused on young men from age fourteen to twenty-five who came from violent and abusive households, providing them needed guidance in life. It also supported those whose families had been ripped apart by drugs and addiction. The organization successfully got the boys off the streets and into apprenticeships and other career programs. Laz had been volunteering for the last few years and wholly supported their mission.

"And to answer your question about me being in a relationship, I am. It's fairly new, but I'm hopeful."

Journey nodded. "Well, I wish you all the best."

Tony's smile grew as he looked past Journey, and she turned to see who had caught his attention. She groaned inside as her college nemesis approached them. Tamar Warner, wearing a gorgeous white suit that hugged her curves, made her way toward them, looking like she had just stepped off the cover of *Vogue*.

No one could ever say the woman wasn't a beautiful sister. Her hair—which was fake—cascaded down in waves over one shoulder. The style accentuated her ebony face that looked professionally made up, and her confident walk snagged just as much attention as Journey's had when she walked in.

Tamar's steps faltered when she saw Journey, but she quickly recovered. She plastered on that familiar fake smile, the one she used when she was in the public's eye as a city councilwoman. Journey saw her out and about more lately since she was gearing up to run for the US Senate.

"Hey, boo," Tamar said, stepping around Journey and placing a quick kiss on Tony's lips.

Interesting. Journey hadn't seen that coming, but considering the way Tony lit up at the sight of Tamar, he was definitely taken with the barracuda.

"Journey, it's been a while," Tamar said by way of greeting, looking her up and down. "You look...the same."

Journey laughed. She wouldn't have expected any other comment from the woman. Tamar had always been jealous of her. They had attended law school together, and there was always some not-so-friendly competition between them. And while Journey had gone on to pass the bar, as far as she knew, Tamar never did. Instead of going into law, she opted for politics.

"Oh, and don't worry, I'm not making moves on your *boo*," Journey said, struggling not to laugh. The term of endearment wasn't one she used often, but its false trendiness seemed to suit Tamar. "And on that note, I'd better get to my friends. Tony, it's always great seeing you."

"Same here, Journey," Tony said with his arm around Tamar. "Oh, and I hope to see you and Laz at the *Save Our Boys* fundraiser Saturday."

"We'll be there," she said and turned to leave, unsure if that was true.

Laz wasn't a big black-tie-affair type of person, but that was one event they usually attended annually. They had their tickets, but right now, she wasn't sure of much when it came to her and Laz.

Finally, she reached Dani's office. They probably would've used one of the party rooms, but Dani had already rented them out. Instead, she offered up her office. Journey hadn't cared where they met as long as there was alcohol and food. She was craving both.

She knocked before pushing the door open, and the scent of oregano, garlic, and a host of other spices made her mouth water. Dani and one of the servers were serving dishes filled with barbecue wings, baked ziti, Caesar salad, and garlic bread.

As if on cue, Journey's stomach growled.

"Hey," she said as she entered. She was getting ready to close the door behind her but spotted Egypt rushing toward it.

"Hey, ladies. Come on in," Dani said, giving her a hug before turning to Journey. "How you doing?"

"I'm hanging in there." Journey hugged her back. "Thanks so much for hosting the impromptu get-together. I really appreciate it."

"Glad to do it. I know if it was me, you'd do the same."

That was true. One thing about their small group, they were there for each other whenever needed. Dani was new to the wives' club, but she had fit in immediately.

"I hope you're hungry. We have plenty of food, wine, and even some hard liquor, just in case."

Hamilton's wife, Dakota, and Angelo's wife, Zenobia "Zen" strolled in a few minutes later. As they all fixed their plates, conversation flowed easily. The stress that Journey had been carrying around for the last twenty-four hours started to fall away. She was so grateful for her sister-friends, her tribe, and she was glad that they could come together.

"Sorry I'm late, ladies," London, Mason's wife, said as she

entered the office. "My little one didn't want me to leave and used all of her tricks to try and get me to stay home."

London, known as "Tiny" to her husband, breezed in wearing a soft pink sweater under a denim jacket and hip-hugging blue jeans with a pair of pink stilettos. She definitely didn't look like a mother of five. Journey didn't know how she managed. The woman couldn't have been more than 5'3" and a hundred and twenty pounds, but the stay-at-home mom ran her household like a pro.

After hugging everyone, she sat at the table next to Journey. "How are you holding up?" she asked.

"I'm all right. I appreciate you guys coming out tonight. I just needed some sister love."

"Girl, we should be thanking you," Dakota said, pouring more wine into her glass. "It felt good leaving the kids with Ham. Although I'm sure by the time I get home, the house will be a wreck, and at least one of them will have a tummy ache."

Hamilton and Dakota had two kids under three and a fourteen-year-old son from Hamilton's first marriage. Dakota was another amazing lady. The former stuntwoman was a total badass with a black belt in tae kwon do. While raising kids and running her household, she owned and operated a dojo and taught self-defense classes.

As Journey glanced around the table, she wondered how all of her friends managed to balance family time and a career. They made it look so easy, rarely missing cookouts, birthday parties, or anything that involved their Supreme family. Yet, she acted as if she couldn't even take time to spend with a husband and daughter she loved to death.

"I need you to tell me your secret," Journey said before thinking. She was embarrassed that she was the only one who couldn't seem to do it all. "I don't know how to balance work and family."

Egypt snorted. "You only see what I want you to see. I can't tell you how many days in a week I go home and feel like I just can't do anything else. No dishes. No laundry. And don't even get me started on sex. I love my big man to death, but he already knows that I'm not giving up the cookies every night."

Dakota chuckled. "And girrrl, don't get me started. Being a wife, mother, and businesswoman means I juggle a lot of balls on a daily basis. Trust me when I say I drop more balls than I keep in the air. There are days when I don't know if I'm coming or going, and I can't tell you the number of times I wanted to run away from home."

They all laughed at that, including Journey. She hated the idea of anyone struggling with responsibilities like she was, but she had to admit it felt good to hear she wasn't alone.

"Well, since Geneva isn't here, I'll pretend I'm her," London said with a wicked grin, and Journey rolled her eyes. They all knew her sister would be talking plenty of trash.

"I'm not sure I want to hear it," Journey said.

London's grin grew larger. "Too bad, because someone has to fill the spot of talking crazy. Let me see, what would she say...." London tapped a manicured finger against her chin. "Oh, I know, she'd say *fuck* his brains out, and if that doesn't work, sit on his face."

Everyone roared. That was exactly what Geneva would say, probably word for word.

"If only that was the problem," Journey said when she finally stopped laughing. "Interesting enough, our sex life is amazing. My problem is trying to juggle work and family. Just when I feel like I'm handling everything, I get bombarded with work, and then my home life suffers."

"Yeah, you have been missing out on a lot of family time," Dakota said.

Journey was sure she wasn't only talking about home life

but also Supreme's family. They were all just as close as if they were blood relatives. Now that she was thinking about it, she was closer to the wives than some of her cousins. They were a lifeline of sorts.

Yet, lately, she'd chosen work over all of them.

The thought was jarring, sending her heart plummeting to her feet.

"I have to do better," she said, rubbing her temples. "I can't keep going like this. Otherwise, I'm going to lose everyone I love. Laz has already lost hope. He might even leave me."

Dakota wrapped her arm around Journey's shoulders. "He's not leaving. He might be a little upset now, but he'd be miserable without you. We know that, and he does, too. Just talk to him. You guys can come up with some type of compromise and then get back on track."

"We've tried, Dee. This is all on me. He does his part. I'm the one who can't seem to get my act together."

"Same," Zenobia piped in. "I don't have half as many responsibilities as the rest of you, and there are days when I don't feel like I know what I'm doing. And now that we're having a baby, I'm scared to death that I'm going to screw everything up."

"Wait!"

"What?"

"You're pregnant?"

"You sneaky little...."

Everyone spoke up at once, laughing and hugging her, genuinely thrilled for her and Angelo. The ladies lost it all over again when they learned that the couple was having twins.

Their Supreme family was growing. Seemed every year someone was having a baby.

London reached over and squeezed Zenobia's hand when the woman looked as if she was going to break down.

"You're going to be an amazing mommy, and when life gets tough, and it will, you have all of us to lean on."

"And just think, you already have built-in aunties and babysitters," Journey said, hugging Zen again.

"They're right," Egypt said. "You can always count on us to have your back. As far as feeling as if you don't know what you're doing, we've all been there, sometimes on a weekly basis," she said with a laugh. "But no one ever said adulting would be easy. Then you add in parenting and trying to have a successful career, and it's easy to get overwhelmed. All you can do is hang in there, and don't be afraid to ask for help."

"And don't feel like you have to be perfect," Dakota added. "That's when shit really hits the fan."

They all laughed as they reclaimed their seats.

More of the tension and stress Journey had been feeling for the last few months continued to wane. She had to remember that she wasn't some superwoman who could or had to do it all. There were times when she should've asked for help, especially at work, but didn't.

Yep, there were definitely going to be some changes. She just had to figure out where to start.

"I'm so glad you guys are saying all of this. I can totally relate," Dani said as they went back to eating and drinking. "After two broken engagements, I had given up on the idea of marriage and having a family. I thought that opening my heart to Ashton was the scariest thing I'd ever do, but when the kids came along, I knew I was wrong. Caring for two preschoolers and running a business is scary as hell."

Again, laughter floated around the room as they all shared mommy stories. As Journey listened, she realized that she definitely wasn't alone. They all experienced moments of being overwhelmed and dropping balls that they were juggling. Still, she didn't have the answers she needed to know what to do next.

"I don't know how to pull my marriage back together," she blurted.

In addition to her law degree, she had a degree in public affairs. Yet, she couldn't keep her husband happy and her marriage together.

Journey lifted her glass of wine to her mouth but stopped. "It's hard to be home by five with dinner on the table and attend family events when I sometimes put in eighty-hour work weeks."

"Why do you do it?" Zenobia asked.

'Why do I do what? Work?"

"Why do you feel like you have to put in eighty hours? I can't even imagine what all goes into trying cases, but is it worth it?"

Journey stared at her friend, then blinked several times before setting her glass back on the table as she pondered the question.

"While you're thinking about that, think about what's most important to you in your life," Egypt said.

"My family is my life," Journey said without hesitation, even surprising herself. It was a no-brainer. She couldn't imagine living without Laz and Arielle, as well as her immediate family and those around the table.

"Then you know what you have to do," Dakota said, filling shot glasses with the tequila that no one had touched.

Journey looked at her friend, wondering if she was saying what she thought she was saying.

"Don't look at me like that," Dakota said, handing everyone except Zen a glass. "You don't need us to tell you that you work too damn much. I get that you want to be the best at your job. Hell, you are the best, but Journey, at some point, you have to ask yourself. Is it worth it? Is putting in an obscene amount of hours at work worth it in the big scheme of things?"

"I remember when I decided to give up touring," Zenobia said, holding up her water glass for Dakota to refill it. "I loved making music, and I loved my fans, but the stress that went with being in the public's eye and touring was too much. It was either continue doing it or live a miserable life. I chose happiness." Though Zen no longer put out records, she still performed on occasion and wrote songs for other musical artists.

"In the words of Geneva...." London said, and everyone laugh-groaned. "Fuck that job! You need to go home and take care of your man."

Everyone burst out laughing, and Journey swatted London's arm. It wasn't just that she had Gen's words down pat, but she even sounded like her.

Journey knew what she had to do. First, she needed to regain her husband's attention...and his trust.

Chapter Thirteen

Laz dragged his tired body up the stairs leading to the crash room he was using at Supreme Security.

His body ached.

His mind whirled.

His emotions were all over the place.

He wanted nothing more than to fall face-first into bed and sleep for a week. Which was what he should be doing, but how could he? He couldn't possibly let the people gunning for him win. That would be unacceptable and not the way he operated.

An eye for an eye.

It was only fair for those involved to experience the pain that he had endured. The fear of not knowing if his child and wife were safe. The horror of watching a young man who had turned his life around bleed out in front of him.

Yeah, somebody was going to pay.

Laz had just left a meeting with Mason, Ashton, and Parker to discuss what they knew so far regarding the gunmen, which wasn't much. Technically, it had been too late in the day for anyone to be gathering, especially on a Sunday night. But that's what friends did, even if there wasn't good news to share.

At least there had been one high point in the conversation. Laz had learned that the day before, Hamilton had called in his own favors to keep Laz's name out of the press.

The media would've eaten up news about a former Atlanta PD detective who now worked for a security agency involved in a fatal shooting. Thanks to Ham, there had been nothing in the news about the incident.

At least not yet.

One thing about Hamilton and Mason was that they protected the people who worked for them, and also did whatever was necessary to protect the stellar reputation of the agency.

Outside of that, the last two days had been a bust.

Laz gripped the stairwell railing, pushing himself to make it up the second flight of stairs though he was bone weary. It had been a long-ass day.

After finding nothing in the stolen vehicle that morning, he, Parker, and Ashton started reaching out and hunting down their personal contacts around the city. His Supreme brothers were amazing at finding answers, but Laz had to tap into some of his other sources every now and then. In other words, those who were connected to the illegal shit on the streets of Atlanta.

People like C-Dogg. Working with them was the only way he'd be able to find the shooters before the cops did.

Otherwise, he'd miss his opportunity to inflict the worst type of justice on those responsible. He wouldn't hold back but planned to stop just short of killing them. Because the last thing he wanted was for his ass to end up back in jail.

Mason's parting words rattled inside Laz's mind before they left the meeting minutes ago.

I want you to let the cops handle this case going forward, and I also want you to take some time off. You got lucky with the bullet not hitting any arteries or doing any major damage. But you're no good to anyone if you don't let that shoulder heal. Besides, I don't need you getting into any legal trouble—or worse.

"I just won't get caught," Laz mumbled under his breath as he trudged up the last few steps. "I should've taken the damn elevator."

He reached the landing and pulled open the door to the hallway. When he turned the corner too short, he bumped his shoulder, and a sharp pain pierced through him like a serrated knife scraping against his bones. His breath caught.

Shit.

He leaned forward, gritting his teeth, waiting for the pain to ease. So much for the pain pill he'd taken a short while ago. The wound hurt like someone had branded him with a hot poker.

Seconds ticked by before he stood upright and readjusted the sling holding his arm in place. Moving again, he continued down the hallway.

The moment he reached the door, a sudden need to go home enveloped him like a tight band around his chest.

He knew what that was about. The idea of sleeping without Journey made him physically ache inside. He didn't sleep well without his wife next to him.

Still, Laz pushed open the door, knowing their temporary separation was for the best.

He stepped across the threshold, and the scent of barbecue had him pulling up short just inside the door. The enticing aroma reminded him that he hadn't eaten since lunch and was suddenly hungry.

Unable to see anything in the darkened room, he flipped on the light switch. The lamps on the side tables provided enough illumination for him to see Journey curled up in a ball on the bed.

Laz's pulse beat a little faster and hammered in his ears. The exhaustion and pain from moments ago were all but gone.

His wife had come to him.

That thought had his heart turning over in his chest, and he would be lying if he said he wasn't glad to see her. He missed the hell out of her. Not because he hadn't seen her since early that morning, but because of the tension that had them arguing more than talking. That wasn't them. That's not how they usually communicated, and that wasn't what he wanted for their future.

I want what we had.

Kenton had been giving him updates throughout the day about her, but seeing Journey with his own eyes brought a level of peace that Laz hadn't felt all day.

Yeah, he was happy to see her. They might have their issues, but his love for her was as strong as ever. He needed to get his head out of his ass and figure out how to fix whatever the hell was broken between them.

Journey's light snores met his ears, and his gaze swept the length of her, taking in her shapely form in a red sweater dress. Her long legs were bare, and he wanted to go over and run his hand along her soft skin and not stop until he reached the sweet spot between her thighs.

He groaned at the thought and shook his head. Sex wouldn't fix their relationship but damned if he wasn't craving his wife.

Instead of waking Journey, he grabbed the duffel bag sitting on the floor near the door, the one he had dropped off earlier, and went into the bathroom. It was a hassle taking a shower and trying not to get the bandage wet, especially since he didn't feel up to changing it, but he made it work.

Twenty minutes later, he had showered and slipped into a pair of navy-blue sleep pants. No way would he be able to get a T-shirt over his head. Instead, he just put the sling back on. He could barely keep his eyes open as he grabbed his two cell phones and left his bag in the bathroom.

Stepping into the bedroom, Laz stopped when his gaze collided with Journey's.

"Hi," she said, her voice low and thick with sleep. She looked as tired as he felt.

"What are you doing here?" he asked.

His body tightened with need as she stood and slowly moved toward him. Seeing how the dress hugged her figure, bringing attention to her pebbled nipples, it was clear that she wasn't wearing a bra.

Laz swallowed hard as she ran her hands down the sides of her body and smoothed her short dress as if self-conscious. Strands of her thick hair had come loose from the ponytail on top of her head and were sticking out, but it didn't detract from her beauty.

Between the hair and her face scrubbed free of makeup, she definitely had that sexy *I-just-woke-up* thing going on, and her natural beauty stole his breath.

"I can't sleep without you next to me," she said, mirroring his thoughts from a little while ago. Her words were almost funny, considering she'd been sound asleep when he'd walked in.

She eased toward him, and his dick stirred the closer she got. Now that she was there, looking sexy in red, he probably wouldn't be able to fall asleep anytime soon.

"I also came because we need to talk."

Laz shook his head. "No. Not tonight, Jay. I'm all talked out, and I can't handle another argument right now."

"I know—me either. That's why I'm going to do the talking, and you'll for-real listen this time. Have a seat." She pointed at one of the chairs at the small bistro-like table near the single window.

Instead of arguing, Laz did as she said and almost laughed. He had a love-hate relationship with what he referred to as her lawyer tone. He loved how ballsy she was when she had something to say or a point to get across like she was questioning someone on the witness stand. That didn't keep him from hating when she used the tone on him.

Laz set the phones on the table. He pulled the chair out and turned it to face her before sitting down.

"I love you," she said as she eased even closer. "I love you more than I did the day I agreed to marry you, and I'm going to love you until the day I die. I know you don't want to hear it again, but I'm sorry for taking you and our marriage for granted. And I'm sure you don't want to listen to promises that I'll get my act together and remember what's most important to me—you and Arielle.

"But Laz, I really am sorry. If I could have a do-over for yesterday, I'd take it in a heartbeat. I was horrified by what you and Ari went through. I can only remember one other time in my life when I'd been as scared as I was hearing the news—and that was when I was kidnapped."

Laz shuddered inside as memories of that time flooded his mind. Terrible regrets would haunt him to the end of time, knowing that someone had taken her. They had planned to do harm to her because of him. She might've only been scared at the time, but he'd been terrified that he wouldn't find her. That he wouldn't see her again.

Journey stopped directly in front of him.

"The only thing that helped me stay calm during that time was knowing that you would find me. There was no doubt in my mind. You'll never understand how horrible I felt yesterday when I wasn't there for the man who holds my heart. Please forgive me for not being there when you needed me. I swear that will *never* happen again. I will do anything to make things right between us, even quit my job."

She said the last part quietly, but Laz didn't miss the conviction in her eyes or her tone. He would never ask her to leave a career that meant the world to her. It brought her joy to help get criminals off the streets, and she was damn good at it. No way would he ask her to quit.

Tears filled her eyes and his gut twisted.

"Will you ever be able to forgive me?" she asked in a small voice, the bravado from moments ago gone. "Just tell me what it will take. I can't lose you."

Laz stood and reached for her. She hurried forward and leaned into his good side, and he tightened his arm around her waist.

"You will *never* lose me," he said quietly and kissed her. "I love you too damn much."

She sniffed and leaned back to look at him. "I love you too, and I can't tell you enough how sorry I am. I hate myself for not being there when you and Ari needed me."

Laz pulled her back against him. "I know." He had known that yesterday, but he'd been overwhelmed with anger. "I don't want you to quit your job. This city and the legal system need you too much."

She didn't respond but tightened her arms around his waist and laid her head on his chest. They stood that way until exhaustion started to get the best of him. He knew they probably needed to talk more. So instead of suggesting they go to bed, he reclaimed his seat and encouraged her to straddle him.

Caressing her cheek with the pad of his thumb, Laz studied her now that she was sitting on his lap. Love twinkled in the depths of her pretty brown eyes, and it felt as if his heart would burst with the love that he had for this woman. Going forward, nothing or no one would ever keep them apart.

"I'm glad you're here." He pushed some of the loose strands of her hair out of her face and let the back of his hand glide over her jawline. "I know we have to figure out how to make us work, but it's not just on you. I'll do my best to be more patient, and we'll determine how to spend more time together without you leaving a job you love."

He punctuated his words with a tender kiss on her kissable lips. He was an idiot the way he'd been behaving lately.

"It's probably been hard to tell, but you're everything to me," he said. "I'm sorry for how I've treated you these last few days. No matter what, I will always love you, Jay, and I'm committed to our marriage."

A tremulous smile tilted the corners of her mouth, and she cupped his face between her soft hands. "Me too," she said, staring into his eyes.

The longer they sat there watching each other, the faster his heart pounded, and his body hummed with need. He might've been exhausted, but Journey had the power to energize him with her nearness. And at this moment, he planned to forget everything else and give his wife his full attention.

He slid his good arm around her waist and pulled her as close to his body as his injured arm, confined to the sling, would allow. Lowering his head, Laz sucked on her top lip, then her lower one, as he held her. He took his time savoring her sweetness while the tender massage of her mouth against his sent currents of desire charging through his body.

He adored this woman. She was so much more than just his wife. She was his best friend. She was his heart.

What the hell had he been thinking when he told her he needed space? There was no way he would've survived more than twenty-four hours without seeing and touching her. She was *it* for him. He couldn't imagine walking through life with anyone else.

Journey moaned into his mouth as her arms went around his neck, careful of his bandages. The kiss deepened as her body melted against him and their tongues tangled to a familiar rhythm. She tasted like tequila with a hint of mint, and he was here for it. That and the intoxicating scent of her perfume had him hard as granite and ready for their bodies to be joined as one.

"I've missed you," he said against her lips before lifting his head.

It sounded a little stupid when he said it out loud, especially since he'd seen her earlier that morning, but it was true. He missed this. He missed having her hugged up against him while sitting on his lap. That was something she often did, climbing on top of him, and he would hold her close.

The position always reminded him of the first time they ever made love...in the tiny kitchen of his one-bedroom apartment.

It seemed like a lifetime ago, but that night they gave themselves completely to each other, after a little debate, of course. His body heated with the memory and how glad he'd been when she had shown up on his doorstep to seduce him.

Laz peppered kisses along the collar of her scented neck. "I hate when we fight."

He ran his hand down the side of her body and slid it beneath the tail of her dress, then froze when he felt her bare ass. Lifting his head, he narrowed his eyes at her.

"Jay, don't tell me you've been walking around town without panties on under this short-ass dress."

A slow, wicked grin spread across her luscious mouth. "I hate when we fight, too," she said evasively, running the pad of her thumb across his bottom lip. "But I'm not wearing panties because I came prepared for us to make up."

Chapter Fourteen

Laz started to laugh at his wife's announcement but groaned when she wiggled on top of him, grinding against his erection. Yeah, he loved that she planned ahead, and he was all for make-up sex, even if he'd have to maneuver with one arm.

"Does this moment remind you of anything?" Journey asked, that grin from a moment ago lighting up her face again.

Laz chuckled. "It does, and I was just thinking about that time when you showed up at my door drunk."

She gasped. "I was not drunk! What I remember most was that you wouldn't give me a little something-something until I agreed to date you exclusively. You've always been difficult, you know that?" she said with a straight face, and he burst out laughing.

"Oh, so because I didn't want you using me for sex, *I'm* the difficult one?"

"Yup, but I'm glad you forced me to date you."

Laz shook his head. "It's amazing how different we remember that time."

He had been crazy about her and wanted her to be his, but he was concerned about his reputation tainting hers. A bad-boy cop who pushed every limit and a by-the-book assistant district attorney didn't look like a good match on paper. But over the years, they proved that they were perfect for each other.

"But seriously," Journey cupped his face between her hands and stared into his eyes, "you're the best thing that ever happened to me, and I'm so glad you're my husband."

"Me too, baby," he said and kissed her sweet lips.

"Is anyone staying in any of the nearby rooms?" Journey asked in a whisper as she sifted her fingers through his hair, something she often did and something he loved.

"Maybe. Does that bother you?"

Laz started lifting her dress higher, needing to see all of her. When he could only get the dress up so far, she helped and tugged it over her head before tossing it to the floor.

"I guess not, but that means you'll have to be quiet."

"*Me?*" He choked out a laugh. "I can't believe you can say that with a straight face. Your passionate screams would wake up our daughter every night if she wasn't such a sound sleeper."

Journey laughed and kissed him. "Okay, I'll try to be quiet."

"Nah, babe, be you. I don't give a damn who hears me making love to my wife."

He was pretty sure there was no one else on that floor, and if there was, they weren't in the rooms on either side of him. Still, he didn't care one way or the other. All he wanted was to be buried deep inside her.

As he took in her gorgeousness, Laz glided his hand slowly down her body from the base of her neck and over her chest, only stopping when he reached her more-than-a-handful breast. "Damn, you're so beautiful," he said, cupping her breast.

She moaned and started to say something, but her words died on her lips when Laz lowered his head and took her nipple into his mouth. Her body trembled as he teased and twirled his tongue around the hardened bud, then sucked it back into his mouth.

With his hand at the small of her back, he pulled her closer, feasting on her flesh as the heady scent of jasmine mixed with citrus made him inhale deeply. Everything about the woman turned him on.

"Laz," she whined.

With the way she was rotating her hips and grinding her sex over his dick, it was clear that he was moving too slow for her. Actually, for him, too, considering he was hard enough to punch a hole through the thin material of his pants.

Moving to her other nipple, Laz readjusted her on his lap and slid his hand between her thighs, finding her clit. Rubbing his thumb over the bundle of nerves, he eased two fingers inside of her slick folds.

"Oh, yes," she moaned, arching into him and moving against his hand.

"Damn, you're wet," he said, nuzzling her neck as he pumped his digits in and out of her heat, working her into a frenzy. As he stirred her passions, his own grew stronger, and his dick grew harder.

"Oh, yes. Right there. Right there," she crooned.

Her eyes were tightly closed as her nails dug into the skin on his upper back while she rocked against him. Laz kept up the pressure. He worked his fingers inside her and his thumb over her clit simultaneously, and when her moves became jerkier, he knew she was close to her release.

"Yes...yes...yes! La...Laz! Ah, yes!" She bucked against him, tightening around his fingers before her body shuddered powerfully as she rode out her orgasm. He loved watching her fall apart like this.

Breathing hard, Journey's eyes were half-closed as she

struggled to get air, then she dropped her forehead onto his shoulder. Laz hissed from the pain before he could stop himself. She quickly lifted her head and turned startled eyes to him.

"Oh, my God. I'm so sorry," she said in a rush and started to get up, but he kept her in place with his hand on her thigh. "Are you okay?" she asked.

"Yeah, but we're not done yet." He clumsily tried readjusting beneath her so he could free himself from his pants. He needed to be inside of her. "This fucking sling. I'm about to rip this.... Dammit, I hate not being able to touch you the way I want to. Maybe we should move to the bed."

"Not yet. Sit tight." Journey lifted slightly. She helped slide the waistband of his pants down, freeing his throbbing dick. "Now...where were we?"

She didn't give him a chance to respond, and Laz inhaled sharply when she lowered herself onto his shaft, never breaking eye contact.

He loved when she took charge, and right now, he was at her mercy as she slid slowly up and down his length. Her interior walls tightened around him, holding him, squeezing him as she showed off just how much muscle control she had. He planned to let her have her way with him.

As if reading his mind, a slow smile spread across her lips, and she picked up speed. He wanted to touch and hold her with both hands as she rode his dick, moving faster and harder, and making him go deeper. Her breast bounced against his chest, sending even more pleasure pulsing through his body.

"Oh...you feel so damn good," he murmured.

Heat hurtled up his spine as he pumped into her, holding her tight with one hand to keep her close as he went deeper. The chair squeaked under their weight, but he was too far gone to care how noisy it was.

"Ah, yeah, baby," he said. Their moves became more powerful and frantic, and Laz tightened his hold around her as he thrust into her harder and faster. "That's it. That's it. That's...ahhh, shit...." A hot flood of passion stormed through his body, rocking him to his core and sending him careening over the edge of control. Journey was right there with him as they came together.

They collapsed against each other. Their chests heaved as they struggled to get air into their lungs.

Journey rested against him, and Laz ignored the pain throbbing through his upper body. He kissed the side of her sweat-slick forehead. "I know I say it all the time, but I'll never be able to get enough of you. But the next time we make love, the sling comes off."

She sputtered a laugh. "Well, considering you were working with one hand, I'm impressed by your skills."

After getting cleaned up in the bathroom, they finally climbed into bed. Journey laid on his good side and snuggled against him. Within minutes, she was sound asleep.

Laz's stomach growled, reminding him he still hadn't eaten the food she had brought with her. But his exhaustion outweighed his hunger, which was his last thought before he finally drifted off to sleep.

A low buzzing stoked Laz awake, and he eased his eyes open. He laid there in the darkness for a few minutes, wondering where the noise was coming from. It stopped, but the moment he closed his eyes again, it started back up.

My phone.

Glad he had moved both devices to the bedside table, he reached over, careful not to wake Journey. If it hadn't been the burner phone ringing, he would've let the call go to voicemail. But there were only a couple of people who had the telephone number, and no way could he ignore the call.

Laz scooped up the device. "Yeah," he said, slowly sitting up on the side of the bed.

"I got something for you," C-Dogg's deep voice boomed through the phone line, sounding like Barry White.

Laz made his way to the bathroom to talk. "Whatcha got?"

"A few guys at Fat Mack's bar were heard bragging about a shooting the other day. They're a couple of bangers, and I'm a hundred percent sure they're who you're looking for. The stupid assholes were debating on which one got off the most shots."

"I need a name," Laz said roughly, his body tightening with rage. He wanted revenge for himself and justice for Nazir, and he planned to get both.

"Shaggy and Baldy," C-Dogg said. "I think Baldy's real name is something like Benny or Henny Madison, but I'm not sure. I do know he lives somewhere in Riverdale. I'll keep digging, but—"

"Don't worry. I'll find them," Laz promised.

Years ago, Atlanta PD had started a database with names of local thugs and gang members. Included were their given and street names. Laz no longer had contacts on the police force who he could call for a favor, but Ashton did.

"One more thing," C-Dogg said. "They think you're dead."

Laz nodded. Anticipation boiled inside of him.

"Good," he said. "They're going to find out that I'm very much alive."

Chapter Fifteen

"You know Mase is going to kill us if he finds out what we're doing," Parker said, slipping on a pair of leather gloves.

It was three o'clock in the morning, and again, Laz had left his beautiful wife in bed to chase a lead. They were sitting in Parker's truck at the end of the block where Benny "Baldy" Madison lived in his grandfather's walkout basement. Perfect for breaching.

After getting the information from C-Dogg, Ashton was able to get names and addresses for Laz. Of course, the information came with a speech. Though his friend understood why Laz had to go after these guys, he thought it was a bad idea for several reasons—the main one being Laz wasn't completely healthy and was going into the situation blind.

He couldn't let that stop him. He needed answers and to send a message to the next person who thought they could come for him without consequences.

"He's not going to find out," Laz finally said as he glanced around. Only having one working arm was a bitch, but it wouldn't stop him from getting a message out. The hard part for him was going to be not killing the bastard who tried to take him out. He had learned that David "Shaggy" Smith had a warrant out for his arrest, but there was nothing on Benny. Before deciding whether to turn Shaggy in, Laz wanted to see if he could get any information from one of the guys. He was starting with Benny since he was the youngest, had no warrants and was new to the 2-7 gang. He'd be easier to break.

"I usually try and stay on the right side of the law, but I have to admit, I'm looking forward to using this thing." Parker turned on the alarm jammer, a device that Laz had picked up from a hacker that he'd busted on more than one occasion. After Laz left the force, he'd kept in contact with The Hackman. He could've asked for Wiz's help, but in situations like this, he tried not to involve Supreme's people in shady shit.

"Ready?" he asked Parker.

Parker had been with Supreme for almost four years and was always up for an adventure. The former Chicago SWAT member had moved to Atlanta with a weapons specialist background. He was one of the most fearless men Laz had ever met. They'd hit it off immediately and worked on numerous assignments together.

"I am if you promise you're not going to kill the guy," Parker said with a laugh, but Laz heard the concern in his friend's voice.

Everyone who knew him well knew that anything was possible. Deep down, Laz wanted to put a bullet between the man's eyes. But Journey's beautiful face came to mind. He never wanted to do anything to disappoint her, and for the most part, he hadn't. This situation was different, though.

"I can't make any promises," Laz finally said and climbed out of the car.

They jogged down the quiet sidewalk, passed a few driveways, and were careful to stay in the shadows. Right away, Laz wanted to yank the sling from around his neck. All it did was piss him off even more that he was hampered by it in the first place.

He definitely planned to take his frustrations out on those responsible. He really needed to be at his best, but because of his injury, he could only do so much. That bugged the hell out of him since he wasn't sure of the skill level of the men they would be dealing with. Maybe he should've got one more person in on this little excursion, but most of his closest friends were married. They all had too much to lose, not that Parker didn't. But out of those Laz trusted explicitly, Parker was the only single one.

They ran up the driveway and around to the back of the house, and Laz cursed under his breath when they saw the fence. Any other time, he would've hopped over it without much thought, but not tonight. Not with only one good arm.

"Hold up," Parker said. With a hand on the wooden fence, he hopped over.

It was three o'clock in the morning, and besides a barking dog in the distance, all was quiet on the block. Laz was counting on the element of surprise to catch Baldy off guard. The last thing they needed was a squeaky gate, especially since, in that neighborhood, it wouldn't be unusual for someone to come out of the bushes with a gun.

Laz moved closer when the gate was unlatched and slowly pushed it open but stopped suddenly when the scraping of metal against metal screeched into the night. When they were sure the noise hadn't alerted anyone, he slipped into the large backyard. For the most part, it was a nice-looking piece of property, except for the second-story deck they were now standing beneath. That deck looked as if a good wind would knock it over.

This is almost too easy, Laz thought when they were at the sliding patio door that had a screen in front of it. To his surprise, the door was partially open, probably for air circulation.

Before going inside, Laz grabbed his cell phone from his jacket pocket and pulled up an app that could record conversations. He had downloaded it weeks ago after hearing some of the guys at work discussing its capabilities. Little had he known that it would come in handy. He wasn't sure what they would learn tonight. But if he could coax a confession out of one of the guys before beating his ass, he'd hand it over to Ted. The thugs would go down for murder and attempted murder.

After starting the recorder, Laz put the phone away and pulled his gun from his back waistband. With the use of Parker's penlight, they eased into the house. As they moved with stealth-like precision, they took in their surroundings. The only illumination in the dimly lit room came from the sixty-five-inch television mounted above the fireplace in a sitting area.

They moved in that direction, their boots silent as they stepped over shoes, clothes, and discarded beer cans while maneuvering through the open space. As they got closer to the TV area, a sofa, love seat, and two recliners sat in front of the fireplace. One of the recliners was occupied by a man in his mid-to early twenties. It was too dark to determine for sure, but Laz assumed it was Benny.

The man didn't move, and they could hear him snoring as they edged closer.

Parker shut off the flashlight, basking the room into darkness except for the light from the television that was muted. They flanked the guy, each standing on either side of the recliner. Baldy held the television remote in one hand, but Laz couldn't see his other hand tucked between his left thigh and the inside of the chair.

He did spot a gun on the table next to the chair and shoved it into his pocket. When he turned over the recording to Ted, he'd also include the gun.

As he stared down at the man who had dared to come after him, anger swirled inside him. The motherfucker could have killed him and Arielle, just like Nazir.

Laz wanted more than anything to wrap his hands around the man's scrawny neck and squeeze the life out of him. First, though, he needed answers.

His gaze traveled the length of Benny "Baldy" Madison, dressed in an Atlanta Braves jersey and jeans. White gym socks covered his feet.

Baldy. What a stupid nickname, considering the guy wore his hair in tiny braids down the back of his head. His fair complexion showed an acne problem, but based on how well-groomed his mustache and short beard were, he took pride in his appearance.

The longer Laz looked at the young punk, the more familiar he seemed, but he didn't know the guy. So why did it feel like he....

The thought screeched to a halt when he remembered where he'd seen the bastard. How the hell had he forgotten about the guys doing a drug deal near his SUV minutes before the shooting? This was one of the guys. After things went down, he had walked in the opposite direction while the other two guys had crossed the street.

Laz's heart rate amped, and he felt Parker shuffle across from him as if sensing something was going on with Laz.

Stay calm. Don't react. Don't fuck this up, he told himself, but it was taking every shred of control to not lift his hand, aim his gun, and blow the man's fucking brains out. Instead, Laz inhaled, exhaled, and willed himself to relax. When he felt some semblance of calm, he nudged the side of the guy's leg.

After a couple of attempts, Benny stirred. His eyes opened slowly, but it didn't seem like he realized he had company.

Laz put his gun against the man's head, and he heard Parker groan before he turned on the lamp on the table next to the chair. Benny stiffened for a second, then started to lunge for the gun he thought was still on the table.

"Don't even think about moving. Your ass thought you could shoot at me and get away with it? Not in this lifetime. Now you're going to answer some questions."

"I ain't telling you shit," the guy spat, trying to sound like he wasn't about to piss his pants.

His words might've sounded fearless, but Laz could feel him trembling. According to the brief dossier that Ashton had texted him an hour ago, the kid had just turned twenty-one. His father was unknown, and his mother was serving five years in prison for assault and battery. Benny had been living with his grandfather since then.

"Well, you either tell me what I want to know, or your grandfather is a dead man," Laz said simply, not missing the way Parker had narrowed his eyes at him.

"Leave him out of this," Baldy said in a rush.

"I guess that means you're ready to talk."

The kid didn't respond, and Laz took that as him being ready to cooperate.

"Why did you target me?" he asked.

When the kid didn't respond, Laz cocked his gun. He didn't want to kill the stupid punk, but....

"Start talking; otherwise, your grandfather will be the least of your troubles," Parker said. "Whoever sent you after my friend here should've warned you that he was crazy. I've stopped him from just outright shooting you, but now you're on your own."

The kid didn't respond, but the pace of his breathing

increased, and the throbbing vein on the side of his forehead was more pronounced.

"Who sent you after me?" Laz had a feeling that this wasn't something Baldy or the other guy came up with by themselves. He'd had no dealings with either of them in the past.

"I don't know," Baldy said, anger lacing his words.

Laz huffed out a breath. "You know what, I'm done being nice. Your ass either start talking, or I'm going to—"

"I'm telling you. I don't know!" Baldy snapped as if he'd forgotten there was a gun pointed at his head. "We got a call, and the deal was to take you out when we got the signal, a text message. I don't know who the person is that called because they used something to make their voice sound mechanical."

"Where's the phone?" Laz asked, glancing around the space, but a phone wasn't in sight.

"It was a burner, and we dumped it."

"Where?" Parker asked. When the guy didn't respond, Parker thumped him hard on the side of the head, and Benny jerked. "I said, where did you dump it?"

Laz listened impatiently to the tale of how this mysterious person communicated with them the day before the shooting. Whoever set the wheels in motion on the hit had thought it through—except for the part of Laz surviving.

"You don't know if it was a man or a woman?" Parker asked.

"No, and I'm telling you the truth. They didn't give us a name."

"How much did they pay you?" Laz asked. This would give him an idea of the socio-economic status of the person behind the hit. "And were you supposed to kill me?"

"Five thousand dollars and yes," the kid said with a sigh.

"What was supposed to happen if you failed? Did you get paid?"

"Yeah. After it was done...or was supposed to be done, we called the number that he gave us."

"He?" Laz and Parker said at the same time.

Baldy shrugged. "I don't know if it was a he. Like I said, his...or her...voice was mechanical. We called him, told him it was done, and he told us where we could pick up the money."

"When and where?"

"That night at a park in Dunwoody off of Shallowford Road near the basketball courts."

Laz frowned. "They didn't ask for proof that I was dead?"

Again, the kid hesitated. "Nah, but he called after we got the money and told us to dump the gun and that we better hope you're dead."

"And if I wasn't?"

"He said you would hunt us down like animals and kill us."

Interesting. The person didn't care if I was dead or not.

Otherwise, they would've wanted proof. This person, whoever they were, also knew him well enough to know that he wouldn't rest until he found the people involved.

I just need to know who. Who'd pay five thousand and not care if I was dead?

That question bounced around in Laz's head, but he still needed more information.

"You keep saying *we*. Who else was involved?" Laz assumed he was referring to Shaggy but wanted to make sure.

The kid hesitated, and Laz pressed the gun harder against his temple. "My patience is spent. So your ass better answer my damn question. Now!"

"I ain't no snitch! I ain't sayin' nothing else. Do what you want to me. I don't care. Just...just don't hurt my grandfather. He had nothing to do with this shit. If you gon' shoot me, go ahead." The kid closed his eyes tightly.

Laz's mind went to Arielle, who was fine and enjoying her

time in Florida, but all he could think about was how terrified she'd been. For that, he wanted so bad to kill the worthless piece of shit.

He glanced up to find Parker staring at him. He was standing in somewhat of a shadow caused by the positioning of the lamp that didn't emit much light. Yet Laz could see the warning in his friend's eyes and feel the intensity bouncing off him.

After a few tense seconds, Laz lowered his weapon and jammed it into the back waistband of his jeans. Then before he could stop himself, he throat-punched the kid, not hard enough to crush his trachea but hard enough to cause pain.

Benny fell forward, holding his neck, gagging, before a coughing fit ensued. Not giving him a chance to catch his breath, Laz pushed Benny's head back against the chair, wrapped his hand around his throat, and squeezed. All he could see were the whites of Benny's eyes.

"If you *ever* come after me again or anyone I know, I *will* kill you. It won't matter whether you're in jail or on the opposite side of the planet. I will hunt your ass down and end your useless life."

"Enough," Parker growled.

Laz jerked his hand away from the man's neck. The move was so violent that it sent Benny falling over the side of the chair and crashing onto the hardwood floor. Benny gasped for air as he tried to get up but fell back to the floor.

Unable to help himself, Laz kicked him in the side of the head and stomped his chest while delivering another verbal warning. Benny lay curled in a ball on the floor, crying in pain.

Good.

Laz headed to the door they had come through. The plan was for him to question Baldy and/or Shaggy, then call Ted to share what he knew. Well, some of what he knew. He'd have to figure out how to erase parts of the recording before handing it over.

If he knew Ted, the detective would continue questioning the thugs, hunt for more answers, and dig for the burner phone which had been thrown in a sewer drain near the basketball court.

By the time the investigation was done, Ted would no doubt wrap it up pretty for the DA's office, and the two punks would end up in jail.

But that still left Laz with a problem. Who the hell was gunning for him?

And there was only one reason the person would pay the money, even though the hit was a bust.

Someone was sending a message....

Chapter Sixteen

Monday morning, as she strolled through the hallways at work, Journey had a little more pep in her step. The weekend had been a roller-coaster of emotions, with the shooting and several arguments with Laz, but as of last night, she felt better than she'd felt in a long time. Sure, she still had a murder case to deal with, but as long as she and Laz were on good terms, she could handle everything else.

"I don't know, Journey. I'm having second thoughts about our agreement from earlier," Angelo said. He and Nelson were her shadows for the day. "Laz wants us to keep you in our sights at all times."

The mention of Laz made her think about how he had snuck back into the crash room just before daybreak. She'd heard him on the phone in the middle of the night, but she had drifted back to sleep before getting a chance to question him about the call. Whatever he'd been up to had gotten him riled up, and he was mentally distracted until they arrived home. Once there, he had showered and fell into bed from exhaustion.

"So, since we can't keep an eye on you from the hallway, we need to come up with a plan."

Journey sighed. This was new territory for her. She wanted to be as cooperative as possible. Especially since Laz was concerned that whoever had come after him might come for her next. Still, she couldn't live inside of a bubble. That was impossible with the type of work she did.

"I know it's not the ideal situation," she said, "but my office deals with highly confidential information. Though I trust you guys completely, you can't just be hanging around."

"How about we make a decision after we see the layout. Then we can have a better idea of what we're dealing with," Nelson suggested. His raspy voice sounded almost like he was a smoker, but according to Laz, the man didn't smoke and rarely drank.

The former US Marshal was older than most of *Atlanta's Finest*, maybe in his early forties, with mahogany skin and buzz-cut black hair with strands of gray peeking out. Slightly over six feet, with broad shoulders and a wide chest, he looked just as intimidating as the others, but he had a calm demeanor.

"What do you say?" Angelo prompted. "We see the layout and then make a decision?"

"That's fair," Journey agreed. "Our suite of offices is through this door." She nodded to her left at the door beside a brass-plated sign on the adjacent wall that read *DA's Office*.

Nelson pulled open the door, and Angelo went in first, then Journey. Once in another short hallway, they flanked either side of her.

"This is our break room." She pointed to a small room to her left that had recently gone through a renovation. The glass walls made the whole area look more spacious, but the increased visibility made it a poor place to relax and get away from people.

As she gave them a quick tour, pointing out the copy room, a few offices, and then the open area that held at least fifteen cubicles.

"There are a few unoccupied cubicles, but we have about ten paralegals and legal assistants who use them," she explained before guiding them to her office area. "My assistant Casey sits at this desk, and my office is just inside here." She unlocked the door to the left and pushed it open.

Both men glanced inside but didn't walk in. They stood a few feet in front of Casey's desk, which overlooked the open space filled with cubicles.

"Okay, so here's what I'm thinking," Angelo said. "One of us will hang out near Casey's desk area, out of the way, and the other will stay near the hallway outside the staff lounge and copy room."

"That could work since the suite isn't as big as I thought it would be," Nelson added. "But is there another exit?"

"There is." Journey pointed to her right. "It's down this aisle, and you'd make a right just past that exit sign hanging on the back wall. We can leave out that way, but no one is allowed to come in through that door."

Both men nodded but didn't look entirely sure about their idea as they continued to look around the open space. They took their job seriously, but Journey was sure they were taking even more precautions because it was her. She was a part of the Supreme Security family, and as Laz often said, family takes care of family.

"Now that we have a plan, we'll let you get to work," Angelo said, and Journey retreated into her office.

Over the next couple of hours, she lost herself in work as she prepared closing arguments for a felony case. She was hoping to finish it before the end of the day, intending to get home at a reasonable hour. Laz told her they needed to squeeze in a date night while Arielle was in Florida. And there was no way Journey would miss dinner out with her husband.

Journey was startled when there was a knock on her office door. She glanced at her watch—or her left wrist where her watch was supposed to be. That was something she still needed to talk to Laz about. She wanted it back. It was one thing to hand it off to Wiz for an update, but she had to make them understand that it wasn't just a GPS device to her. It had been a special gift from her husband that she cherished.

"Come in," she called out and wasn't surprised when Prentice walked in. They were meeting with Joyce Hayes's husband. Detectives had questioned him shortly after his wife's murder in her office at Leverage Construction, but he'd been so out of it at the time. They were hoping they could get more information out of him this morning that might shed more light on her relationship with the CEO, who was accused of murdering her.

"Good morning," she said and pulled out the file for that case. "I've come up with a few questions to—"

"Are we seriously going to pretend that Saturday afternoon didn't happen?" Prentice asked and unbuttoned his suit jacket before sitting in one of the chairs in front of Journey's desk.

Journey pinched the bridge of her nose. "I'm sorry. This was a crazy weekend. I got your voicemail. Thanks for checking in, and I'm sorry I had to text you instead of call you."

"So, what happened? All your text said was that Laz was shot, but he's going to be okay."

She trusted Prentice explicitly, but instead of saying too much, she said, "I can't go into great details right now, but Laz and his team, along with the cops, are checking into it. As soon as I can say more, I'll tell you everything."

Prentice nodded. "And the security detail?"

"That's just Laz being overprotective. Until he knows who's gunning for him, he wants me protected."

The right corner of Prentice's lips lifted into a crooked smile. "And you thought he didn't care about you."

Journey grinned back at him. "Is this you trying to get me to say—*you were right*?"

"I don't need to hear it. I already knew how crazy in love that man is with you. I'm just surprised that you were having doubts."

"Not any longer. We're back on track."

At least, for the most part, she thought.

Once she closed the Dennis Stratton and Leverage Construction case, Journey planned to seriously consider her future in the DA's office. Yes, she would love to make a run for the DA's position after Gaines retired, but not at the expense of her family. She had taken Laz and Arielle for granted, which would never happen again.

A short while later, Journey and Prentice entered the conference room. A man about her age with dark, spiked hair graying around the temples stood when she walked in. The sprinkle of freckles on top of his nose and cheeks stood out against his pale skin. He was around 5'10, with a slim build and a slight beer belly.

"Mr. Hayes, I'm assistant district attorney Journey Dimas," she said, extending her hand and shaking his. "And this is our investigator, Prentice Johnson. Thank you so much for coming in this morning to meet with us. Please, have a seat. Can I get you more coffee or something else to drink?"

"No, this is good," he said, lifting a cup of coffee that Casey had probably given him.

Journey and Prentice sat on the other side of the table across from him. "I'm sure you have plenty to do, and I'll try not to keep you long. We hope you can tell us something that might help our case."

"I'll help any way I can to make sure that monster who killed my wife rots in jail. What do you need from me?"

"First, please accept our condolences. I'm sure this has to be hard on you and your children," Journey said, and immediately her thoughts went to Laz and Arielle.

She could be the one on the other side of the table answering questions. She was so glad the situation hadn't turned out any worse because instead of being at work, she could be the one planning a funeral.

Shaking the thought from her mind, Journey opened the file in front of her, where she had a few notes. Before she could pose one, Prentice spoke.

"Mr. Hayes, has your wife had any problems with the CEO of Leverage Construction?"

He shook his head. "Not as far as I know. I've been wracking my brain the last couple of weeks, trying to determine if I missed some signs of trouble. I can't believe she's gone," he whispered the last part.

Journey's heart went out to him. They had three grade-school kids who now had to grow up without their mother, and for what? Something so senseless as an argument at work.

"Mr. Hayes," Prentice prompted.

"I'm sorry," he sniffed. "Talking about her in the past tense.... Some days her death doesn't seem real. My sister says I'm in shock, but—"

"Maybe this is too soon," Journey said, putting herself in his shoes. "If—"

"No. I'm sorry. Let's do this. I want to help. Maybe making sure her killer stays behind bars.... Or if he turns out to not be the killer, hopefully, I can say something that can find the real killer. I—I want justice for my wife."

"And you're going to get it," Journey said with conviction. She would do whatever she could to make sure that happened.

"Has she been distracted or upset about anything at work?" Journey asked. Something was going on at that company, and when she found out what, she'd be able to build a solid case against the CEO.

"She was a little stressed the last few months, but I didn't realize she even knew the CEO. As far as I know, he wasn't her direct supervisor. She reported to Marta Polczynski."

Journey scribbled that bit of information on the tablet in front of her. She assumed Marta had been a coworker, not Joyce's supervisor. Marta never said otherwise.

"My wife was always serious about her work, saying that accountants were the backbone to any successful business." Mr. Hayes gave a little laugh. "She was a dedicated employee who hated missing any days."

"Do you know if she had problems with anyone at work?"

The man rubbed his chin for a few minutes and stared at the table while he thought about the question. Journey hoped he could give them something they could use. Anything.

"Actually, a few weeks ago, she mentioned that she might have to find another job because she didn't agree with some of the things her boss wanted her to do. I didn't think much of it because she considered looking for work at a smaller company every few years."

"Did she say what she didn't agree with?" Prentice asked.

"Not really. Actually, maybe she did," he said sheepishly. "When she talked numbers and finances, the conversation was often over my head, and I barely listened. But whatever was going on, she thought it was unethical and not good business practice."

Journey nodded. "I heard from someone else that the

company was in talks with another company about a possible merger. Did Joyce say anything to you about that?"

"She talked about that a few months ago, maybe even a year ago, but she hadn't said anything about it lately. I assumed it wasn't going to happen. Lately, whenever she discussed work, it was mostly about some huge city contract Leverage was hoping to land."

Journey tapped her pen against the yellow legal pad next to her. Money—or the lack of it—could make tempers fly. Maybe the argument between Joyce and the CEO, Dennis Gardner, had something to do with the contract.

"What type of contract?"

"Some type of housing contract for the city of Atlanta. She and a couple of others in her department had to put in some long hours because financial information had to go along with the proposal."

"A company the size of Leverage Construction should've been able to easily pull any information that the city needed, especially financials," Prentice said, but it sounded more like he was talking to himself.

"I think there was some problem with balancing the books, but don't quote me on that. As I said, I didn't listen as well as I should have," he said, his voice cracking on that last part.

When he didn't continue, Journey asked if he needed a minute, but he shook his head *no*. Still, she waited a moment before continuing.

"Did it seem like she didn't want them to be awarded the contract?"

"No, that wasn't it. She said that if the company was awarded the contract, it would take the organization to another level. In the proposal, they had included small and large organizations that the company had been wanting to work with. Or something like that. She seemed excited about it because it would mean raises for her and her coworkers, and the company would expand. That would provide more jobs for people, something Joyce was passionate about."

Prentice stood suddenly and held up his cell phone as he headed for the door. "Excuse me for a minute."

Journey wondered what that was about since he never walked out on an interview, but she had a couple of more questions for Mr. Hayes.

For the next few minutes, she asked more about Joyce. She wanted to get a feel for who she was as a wife and mother.

Mr. Hayes lit up when he talked about her, and Journey's heart broke a little more for him and his family. The more she knew about the woman, the more she could use in court when she went up against Dennis Stratton's attorney, a formidable opponent.

The DA's office just needed a little more evidence to strengthen the case against Stratton. Considering there was still so much that didn't add up, getting a conviction would be easier said than done.

Chapter Seventeen

After showing Mr. Hayes out, all Journey could think about was getting justice. She hoped she'd also be able to give him and his family the closure they needed to heal by the time she closed the case.

As she headed back to her office, she ran into Prentice in one of the aisles.

"What happened?" she asked quietly, and he fell in step with her.

"We need to question Marta Polczynski again. I requested she be picked up by an officer and brought here instead of having her taken to the station for questioning. I really think someone got to her before she talked to us."

Journey nodded. "I agree, and I think it's very convenient that Marta never mentioned that she was a supervisor at the company and that Joyce was one of her direct reports. If someone put the fear of God in her, we'll have to get her to trust us enough to talk. How soon will she be here?"

He glanced at his phone. "Not sure. They're at her house

now, but no one's answering and the neighbors haven't seen her."

An unsettling sensation lodged in the pit of Journey's stomach. She hoped the woman was all right, but after what happened to Fred, she feared the worse.

"Okay. Keep me posted."

When Journey returned to her office, she pulled out her cell phone and called Laz. He hadn't gotten much sleep the night before, and she was concerned that his recovery would take longer with all that was going on. He needed rest. Something he wasn't getting.

"Hey, baby," he said sleepily, and Journey smiled at the tingles that scurried up her spine.

She never thought she'd be the type of woman who got all giggly inside when her man used pet names. Or when his sexy, sleep-filled voice worked her up to the point of wishing she could ditch work, meet him at home, and coax him into bed.

"Are you okay?" he asked.

"Oh...yeah, I'm fine. I was just checking on you. How do you feel?"

"Like I got shot and dragged behind a car for a mile along a pothole-riddled street."

"Laz." Even if part of that was actually true, Journey didn't want a picture painted for her.

He chuckled. "All right, babe. I've been in bed since you left. I knew I was tired. I just didn't realize how much."

He sounded exhausted, and the fact that he was still in bed spoke volumes. Laz was an early riser, and there wasn't a lazy bone in his body. He was one of those people who could function on little sleep and be just as productive as someone who got a full eight hours.

"Where'd you go last night, or should I say this morning? I woke up around three, and you weren't in the room." She had known that it wasn't just the room he had vacated; he had left the building. She didn't know how many clothes he had brought, but when she didn't see his phones and leather jacket, she knew.

After a hesitation, Laz said, "I got a lead on the shooting, and I went to check it out. Nothing for you to worry about, though."

Meaning he probably found someone directly tied to the situation and beat them up—or at least threatened them for information. She hadn't noticed any bruises on his knuckles, but with Laz, even with one arm in a sling, he could do some damage.

When he worked for the police force, Laz constantly pushed boundaries, making her job almost impossible some days. Requesting search warrants without having enough probable cause, going off half-cocked after perpetrators, and basically just doing whatever he saw fit to put bad guys behind bars.

Journey recalled a couple of times when she'd walk into an interrogation room, where a criminal was being held, and they'd be visibly shaken. Not for fear of going to jail, but for fear of the arresting officer—Laz. He always got his man.

"How are you doing?" he asked, cutting into her thoughts. "How's it going with your security detail? Hopefully, they aren't cramping your style too much."

"I'll admit it's taking some getting used to, but I understand the need to have them around."

"I'm glad you understand. Hopefully, it won't be for long. We're going to find the person behind this shit, and then we can return to our lives."

Yeah, she hoped.

"I know you want to find the people who shot at you, but you need to stay in bed and get some rest," she said, thinking about how pale he had looked when she left for work. "I need you to hurry and heal so that you'll have full use of both of your arms and hands."

Laz chuckled. "Yeah, I prefer to use both hands and have a bed beneath me when I make love to my wife. Last night, it felt like I was having sex with one arm tied behind my back."

Journey couldn't stop the grin from spreading across her face. "I imagine it did, but it was still fun." She laughed. "I can't wait to do it again. Chair and all. As a matter of fact, maybe tonight we can have a repeat of last night. Wait, what am I thinking? I'm sure we can get creative where you won't even need your hands. Actually, maybe I'll just have my way with other parts of your body."

Laz groaned. "Damn, I love the way you think. Uh, so when are you coming home?"

They both laughed, and it felt good. Arguing with him wore her out; lately, that was all they'd been doing. It seemed like they were finally turning the corner to get their marriage back on track.

"I'm planning to leave here at six. I would suggest we have a date night and go to dinner, but I'm not sure that's a good idea," Journey said. If someone really was after Laz, going to a restaurant would only put others at risk.

"Yeah, we should probably lay low. How about I order us a nice dinner and make sure it's here by the time you get home?"

Journey smiled, and warmth spread through her body. "That sounds great."

"Good, I'll see you later then," he said.

"Okay, and Laz?"

"Yeah?"

"I love you."

"I love you too, sweetheart. And don't give my guys too much trouble."

Journey laughed. "I can't make any promises, but I'll try."

* * *

Still smiling after her call with Laz, Journey opened her bottom desk drawer and pulled her makeup compact from her purse. Looking in the small mirror, she patted away the sheen from her face, freshened her brick-red colored lipstick, and had put everything away when Prentice showed up in her doorway.

"What's up?" she asked and rocked back in her seat.

"Marta's here, and she was getting ready to run."

Journey sat forward, frowning. "What? What do you mean? Running from what...or who?"

"That's what we need to figure out. I'm thinking we should meet in your office."

"Oh, okaaay." Journey wasn't sure why he was acting so strange, but when he escorted Marta in, she saw why.

The other day, the woman's blonde hair was in a fancy updo, and her face looked professionally made-up. She'd been dressed in a nice blouse and pants. Yet, right now, her hair hung loose beneath an Atlanta Braves baseball cap that she had paired with a ratty sweatshirt, paint-spattered blue jeans, and a pair of blue Chucks.

The outfit looked like a disguise, and with the large, multi-colored overnight bag slung over her shoulders, she looked as if she was getting ready to run away.

Concern engulfed Journey as she slowly walked around the desk.

"Ms. Polczynski, I'm glad you're here. Please, have a seat." Journey gestured to one of the guest chairs in front of her desk.

"It's not like I had a choice," she snapped and dropped into the chair as if she was tired from carrying a heavy load. Not only was her appearance different, but so was her attitude.

Prentice sat in the chair next to her, and Journey returned to her seat.

"Why was I brought here instead of the police station?" Marta asked.

Journey propped her elbow on the desk and rested her chin on her hand. Now she knew something was going on; it was as if the woman had been expecting to get arrested. "Would you have preferred to be at the police station instead of here?"

She didn't answer the question right away, and for a minute, Journey didn't think she'd respond until she said, "Maybe I should have a lawyer present."

"Why? Did you do something wrong?" Journey asked.

The woman didn't respond, which told Journey what she already knew. Marta was involved in the murder in some way. Or at least she knew more than she'd let on the other day, and now she was running scared.

"The cops found you at the bus station. Why were you leaving town?" Prentice asked. "Where were you heading?"

A flicker of fear showed in the woman's eyes, but it was gone just as fast. Now they were getting somewhere.

Journey leaned back in her seat and tapped her pen against the yellow legal pad on the desk. She stared at the woman who was looking down, fiddling with the handle of her large bag.

"You know, Marta, if you prefer, we can always have you transported to the police station for additional questioning," Journey said, hoping that would get her attention. "With you lying to detectives and then lying to us, legally, things aren't going to end well for you."

Journey let that sink in. According to the eyewitness statement, Fred—their murdered key witness—had stated Stratton was the one who actually killed Joyce.

But where did Marta figure in?

"Or you can stick around," Journey continued. "We can

just...have a conversation. I'm not sure what your role is in all of this, but maybe there's a way we can help each other. What do you think?"

After a slight hesitation, Marta glanced up and met Journey's eyes. "What do you want to know?"

"Why were you leaving town?" Prentice asked again.

"Because...I think I'm in trouble, and I need protection."

Journey frowned and sat forward. "Excuse me? Protection from what or who?"

"I don't know. I'm scared. The crap going on at Leverage might get me killed like it did Joyce and Fred."

"Why do you say that? Do you know something we don't know? Because when we talked to you days ago, you said—"

"I know what I said!" she snapped, then covered her face with her hands. "I'm sorry. I'm just...I'm just really stressed."

Journey moved around the desk and propped against the corner closest to Marta, hoping to make her feel more comfortable.

"Tell us why you were trying to leave town."

"The killings. I've watched enough crime shows to know that Joyce's and Fred's murders only weeks apart is too much of a coincidence."

"Okaaaay," Prentice said slowly. "Do you know why they were killed?"

"At first, I thought it had something to do with the merger. But now I think it might have something to do with the city contract that we were just awarded. Except...I don't know. I'm not sure."

Journey exchanged a look with Prentice. He was probably thinking the same thing she was thinking. The proposed merger and the mention of that city contract had come up twice in the past hour. From what she understood, the merger had fallen through over a year ago.

Still, Journey wanted to ensure she did her due diligence and investigated. That went for the contract, too. There was probably some information in one or the other that could shed light on the whole case.

"I think Joyce might've been murdered because she threatened to go to the authorities about us manipulating the financial records," Marta said in a rush, as if she had to get the words out before changing her mind. "It was wrong. I know it was wrong, but we were told to do it or we'd lose our jobs."

"Who is we?" Journey asked.

"Me and my team, which included Joyce and Shawn Ridley."

Journey jotted Ridley's name down to remind herself to see what they had on him.

"Before discussing a merger, Dennis wanted us to make changes to the company ledger. We were forced to keep two sets of financial records. The real set, and another set that was used to get loans and lure investors. He *insisted* we hide some of the debt he'd been accumulating and add revenue that didn't exist.

"At first, it was small amounts that were easy to conceal, but over the last few months, the amounts were getting too large to hide. I was concerned that either the potential investors would request an audit or the city would. We have had several large city contracts over the years, and it's not unheard of for them to do that."

"So basically, he wanted the business to look more profitable than it actually was," Prentice said.

Marta nodded and released a heavy exhale. "I've been with the company almost ten years, and we used to do everything by the book. Dennis was an honorable man. That's how the company kept growing. People trusted our brand and us."

"Why did you lie to us and try to make it seem like

Leverage Construction was a great place to work?" Journey asked.

"Because I didn't want to get in trouble. I didn't know what would happen if you or the detectives discovered that the company was committing fraud." She swiped tears from her eyes. "Leverage was doing well at first, but then a couple of years ago, a major contract that Dennis was banking on fell through, and it seemed like a snowball effect. He was losing other deals."

Journey wasn't sure the information the woman shared was worth killing over. Yes, it looked bad that Dennis had manipulated his employees into fudging the books...but murder?

"When we were awarded this new city contract a few weeks ago," Marta continued, "I thought for sure we could start operating the way we used to, but then Dennis had to start paying the councilwoman more than he could actually af...." Marta gasped and slammed her hand over her mouth.

"Wait."

"What?"

Journey and Prentice spoke at the same time. Journey was on her feet, standing in front of the woman who looked as if she was going to bolt.

"I shouldn't have said anything. Forget I said anything," Marta stammered and stood, grabbing her bag from the floor. "I have to go. I can't—"

"Sit down, Marta," Journey said firmly. "You're not going anywhere until you give me a name. What city council member are you claiming has been taking bribes?"

Marta looked from her to Prentice and back to Journey again. She swallowed hard before saying, "Councilwoman Tamar Warner."

Chapter Eighteen

Journey laid her head back against the bath pillow and closed her eyes. Soft jazz filled the bathroom, candles flickered from every flat surface, and she savored the calming feeling of the bubble bath that Laz had surprised her with.

Heaven. That's what it was. Pure heaven.

They had renovated their huge master bathroom when they purchased the home a few years ago. Now it had all the luxuries—heated floors, marbled tile, a double-wide steam shower, a glorious, free-standing tub big enough for two, and the list went on. Still, she could count on one hand how often she got to soak in her tub.

That was just depressing. She worked her ass off every day, made an amazing living, and didn't make time to enjoy the fruits of her labor.

"That's going to change," she mumbled to herself, meaning every word.

She had arrived home tonight from work at exactly six o'clock. It was sad that she couldn't remember the last time she'd gotten home before eight. Even then, she often brought work with her, but not tonight. Laz had been adamant that their date night be a work-free zone, and she was all for it.

Instead of eating dinner right away as she had expected, he'd had a snack prepared for her. Cheesecake bites. She smiled at the memory. He'd insisted that she deserved to have dessert before dinner, and all she could do was laugh at the idea. Even as an adult, she had difficulty allowing herself to eat dessert first. It had been an ongoing joke between them.

Sighing, Journey settled deeper into the warm water and bubbles that stopped just below her chin. Immediately, her thoughts went to the conversation with Marta.

Tamar Warner accepting bribes?

It didn't make sense. Journey still couldn't wrap her brain around that, assuming Marta was telling the truth, and that was a big assumption. The woman had lied more than once after her coworker was killed. Who was to say she wasn't lying now?

But why would she lie? What would she have to gain by saying Tamar—a city councilwoman loved by the people of Atlanta—was accepting bribes?

Then again, when it came to Tamar, anything was possible. The woman was condescending, entitled, and definitely the jealous type. She'd also do whatever she had to do to win at anything, but Journey had never known her to break the law. Heck, the woman knew the law better than anyone.

Journey eased her eyes open as a thought occurred to her. "Which also means she'd know how to break it without getting caught."

Then there was Marta.

Journey shook her head and let her eyes drift close again.

After questioning the woman and wanting to believe what she was sharing, Journey had arranged for a squad car to sit outside of Marta's house temporarily. At least for a couple of days until she could find proof to prove the woman's claims. If what she told them was true, Journey could make the case that protective custody was needed, seeing Marta would be a key witness.

And if her claims about Tamar were correct, the Feds would have to be notified. A public figure accepting a bribe was a federal offense.

What a mess.

Journey might not like Tamar, but she hated thinking that the woman would risk everything...and for what? A few dollars? Favors? If the accusation was correct, not only could she kiss her job and the possibility of becoming a US Senator goodbye, but she could also expect to spend some time in jail.

Oh, no. Tony....

"Jay? Tell me you didn't fall asleep," Laz said from somewhere in the bathroom, and Journey smiled.

She opened her eyes just as he sat on the upholstered stool next to the tub.

"I think I love you," she said wistfully, feeling totally relaxed despite the route her mind had taken.

Laz laughed. "Well, I should hope so since you're stuck with me."

He kissed her lips, then boldly cupped her breast, caressing and teasing her pert nipple. Journey couldn't stop the moan from slipping through. His nearness and his touch had desire swirling inside her, and her head fell back against the bath pillow.

This man. This sweet, sexy, badass man knew how to turn her on.

"I came in here to tell you that dinner is ready, but now that I'm here, I'm thinking maybe I should help you relax a little more before we eat."

He slipped his hand into the water. Like a heat-seeking

missile, he found his way to the apex of her thighs. Journey sucked in a breath and arched her back when he slipped a finger inside her. Between his thumb and fingers touching, teasing, pinching, and basically driving her crazy, she couldn't help squirming in the water.

"Goodness. You were right the other day when you said there's a lot you can do with one hand," she said with a nervous laugh. "Or maybe I said it. Ohh...."

She nearly leaped out of the tub as he continued stoking the flame burning inside of her. Her legs squeezed together, trapping his hand in place while she struggled to keep breathing. The man's fingers were magical, like a weapon he used to shut her up and keep her in line. That wasn't even an exaggeration. Between the water swishing between her legs, and the way he was picking up speed, sliding his fingers in and out of her, Journey couldn't speak. She could barely think.

One last stroke of his fingers and she fell apart. The toe-curling orgasm had her gripping the sides of the tub tighter as everything inside of her exploded.

"Oh, my...." she panted.

When she glanced up, Laz was smiling. "Well, the first part of this date is going better than I expected." He bent over and kissed her sweetly. "Now, quit messing around, and come on. I don't want the food to get cold."

Journey sputtered a laugh, scooped up a handful of water, and threw it at him. He laughed, dodging most of it before hurrying out of the room.

She sat back, wanting just a few more minutes of relaxation.

God, I love my man.

* * *

Laz was feeling pretty proud of himself. It had been a long time since he romanced his wife. Knowing that the last few days—hell, the last few months—had weighed on her, he wanted to do something special. He wanted to make her feel special because that's what she was to him.

If the shooting had taught him anything, it was that life was short and could be snuffed out in a heartbeat. The days of taking what they had for granted were over.

"Man, this is so good," Journey crooned, moaning as she stuffed a piece of honey-glazed chicken into her mouth. "Thank you for this, and feel free to cook for me anytime."

Laz chuckled. She knew as well as he did that the only part of the meal he'd prepared was the broccoli and garlic bread. He had ordered the chicken, three-cheese scalloped potatoes, and cheesecake bites from her favorite restaurant.

"Only the best for you, baby," he said, bringing his beer bottle to his mouth and taking a healthy swig. Sitting across the candlelit table from her, watching her enjoy the meal, was all the thanks he needed.

He had wanted to take her to her favorite restaurant, but it wasn't safe yet. It was bad enough that they had security sitting outside the house. Going to a restaurant with her would've meant even more guys watching their backs. So, he'd done the next best thing and ordered in. Until they found the mastermind behind the hit, they weren't taking any unnecessary chances.

Thinking about taking chances brought to mind his adventures from the night before. He had handed over the recording once he'd gotten Wiz to clean it up, and the shooters had been arrested. All three were in protective custody at the hospital, recovering from concussions, busted ribs, and a few broken bones. Neither volunteered how they had sustained their injuries, but Laz was sure Ted and Remy knew.

Laz and Parker, after they visited with Benny that night, found Shaggy, the other shooter, and they also found the driver. The two assholes happened to be roommates and lived in an apartment on the east side of town.

After a bit of persuasion, they confessed to their role in the shooting and suffered a similar beating as Benny. It helped that Laz knew enough about their families to use them as a threat to get the punks to talk. It also ensured that they'd keep their mouths closed about how they had sustained their injuries.

Laz had no plans of going after any of their family members, but they didn't need to know that.

Ashton had been a huge help, and Laz would forever be in his debt. His friend had been instrumental in getting the evidence to Ted, making it seem like he got everything from a confidential informant. That included Benny's gun that Laz had confiscated.

A couple of hours ago, he had gotten word that, after ballistics had been run on the weapon, the data confirmed that it was the weapon used in Laz's shooting and matched a homicide case from two months earlier.

Needless to say, the three punks would spend the rest of their lives in jail.

Journey set her fork down and wiped her mouth with a napkin. She smiled at Laz over the tapered candles that had melted down to stubs, and his heart squeezed at the love he saw in her gaze.

"I can't remember the last time I felt this relaxed," she said. "Thank you for giving me just what I needed. I always enjoy our date nights, and I promise we'll get back to having them regularly."

He could tell she was still feeling guilty about her role in their marital issues, but Laz was more than ready for them to move past any problems. They had both apologized, agreed to do better at putting their marriage first, and that was all he needed. He just had to figure out how to get her past it.

Time. All it would take was time for her to realize they were in a good place.

He reached across the table for her hand. "I have no doubt we're on the right track, but babe, you talk about this being a relaxing evening, and I can tell you've been distracted for much of it. What's on your mind?" he asked, caressing the back of her fingers with his thumb. "And before you say nothing, remember, I used to be a detective. I'm good at reading people."

She gave a little laugh and sighed. "I'm sorry. I know you said this is a work-free zone tonight, but I can't stop thinking about this case." She squeezed his hand before releasing it and picked up her wine glass. "It started as a murder case, but it's turning into so much more, including company fraud."

He pushed his chair back and stretched out his legs in front of him, crossing them at the ankle. Laz didn't know much about the case since Journey didn't really discuss it—or any of them, for that matter. But he could tell early on that this one bothered her more than others. That was saying a lot, considering some of the heinous crime cases she took on.

"No, I'm not doing this," she said, shaking her head. "I'm not going to ruin a beautiful evening with my husband to discuss work."

"Babe, if you need to talk it out, we can."

"Thanks, but no. We're on a date, and I'm giving you all my attention."

Laz sat forward and shrugged. "All right, cool. Then let me clean up the kitchen. Then we can go upstairs, and I'll see if there's anything I can do to take your mind completely off work."

A sensual smile spread across her mouth as she stood and sauntered toward him with a seductive swing of her hips. He liked the white shirt dress she was wearing. It was thin, but not quite thin enough for him to see through the cloth. What he loved most was that it provided easy access.

She hiked up the hem of the garment and straddled his lap.

"I was thinking...." She started unbuttoning his shirt, and Laz shook his head.

"No," he said emphatically, despite her moving closer to position herself on top of his dick. "Don't even think about it. We're not doing this in a chair tonight."

He cursed under his breath and tried to ignore how she was grinding against him. Tried to ignore the way her hips moved rhythmically while her hands roamed up his body. And he tried to ignore how incredible she felt.

Damn this woman and her sexy ass when she got like this. She always made it hard for him to....

"Jay," he hissed, his fingers digging into her hip, struggling to keep his body from matching her moves. "I told you, the next time we...."

Her cell phone, which was sitting on the table, rang with her father's ringtone, and Laz stiffened. It was almost ten o'clock at night, and they had already talked to their daughter. There was only one reason Logan would be calling.

"Get it," he demanded, his body going rigid for fear that something had happened to his baby.

Journey leaped from his lap, stumbling in the process, before snatching up the device.

"Dad?" Journey put the phone on speaker. "Is everything all right? Is Ari all right?" she asked in a rush.

"Hi, Mommy," Arielle said, her sweet little excited voice flowing through the speaker. "I saw Princess Tiana today!" she screeched. "And you know what else...."

Laz released a ragged breath and dropped his forehead on the table while trying to get his heartbeat back to normal.

Damn. Damn. Damn. This situation was going to give him a heart attack.

Journey rubbed his back, but the small circling of her hand did nothing to settle his tattered nerves.

He couldn't keep living like this. Living with the fear that someone was going to get to his family. He didn't scare easily, but that was the one thing that scared him to death.

I have to find whoever this person is. And I have to find them soon.

Chapter Nineteen

Laz couldn't remember the last time he'd been in the DA's office, but he did recall all of the debates he'd had with Journey whenever he showed up to request a warrant. She wasn't one to hand them out easily, always asking a ton of questions to decide if he had probable cause to get one.

The thought warmed him from the inside out. If anyone had told him back then that she'd one day be his wife, he would've laughed them out of the room. The woman was so far out of his league, then and now. He never imagined that they'd ever get together, even if he wanted them to. Their relationship was living proof that anything was possible.

Laz readjusted the large white bag of food in his hand and strolled through the hallway past the staff lounge. Before Journey left for work, he had suggested they have lunch together and had been surprised when she agreed. It probably wouldn't be a long meal, but at least they took time for each other.

Actually, he had nothing but time. He finally had a chance

to catch up on sleep since Mason had benched him, and Laz had no more leads on the shooting. And if Ted had anything, he was holding it close to his chest. Laz would bet that they were just as stumped as he was. Whoever was behind the hit had been extremely careful.

"Hey, Laz, it's been a while," one of the paralegals said from her cubicle as he strolled down the aisle that led to Journey's office.

"Yeah, it has. Good to see you, Lynn," he said and kept moving.

He greeted and nodded to a few other familiar faces, either sitting at their desks or walking through the aisles. When he reached Casey, Journey's assistant, she was on the phone but lifted a finger to tell him to give her a minute.

While picking up lunch for him and Journey, Laz had gotten a turkey club and chips for Casey. He sat the small white bag on the corner of her crowded desk and was rewarded with a big smile. Anyone who looked out for his wife was all right in his book. Journey adored her assistant, a paralegal, and Journey often said that she couldn't do her job without her.

Now in her mid-forties, Casey could easily pass for a woman in her thirties, especially with the new hairstyle. She used to wear her hair long, but now the strawberry-blonde strands were cut into a short bob. It fit her and made her blue eyes seem even bluer.

"Hey, Laz. Sorry about that," Casey said when her call ended. She grabbed the lunch bag. "And thank you so much for the sandwich. Journey mentioned that you would bring lunch, and I really appreciate it. This saves me from ordering in searching for food later."

"No problem."

She frowned and nodded toward his sling. "What happened to your arm? Is it broken?"

"Nah, just had a little mishap." Apparently, Journey hadn't told her assistant about the shooting, so Laz decided he wouldn't either.

"Hopefully, it's nothing too serious."

She told Laz about the time her youngest son was pretending to be Superman and decided to fly down the stairs. He'd ended up with a broken arm and a mild concussion.

"Look at me yammering on. Journey texted and said that she's in the building and should be here shortly. She said for you to go on in. Oh, and I think it's great that you got her some personal security. I know she wasn't taking the threats seriously, but...."

Laz froze, and his mind locked on the word *threats* while Casey kept chatting.

What the hell?

"Hold up. What threats?" he ground out, trying to keep his shock and simmering anger at bay. How could Journey not tell him that she was being threatened? Granted, he knew it came with the job, but still...she should've said something.

Casey's wide-eyed gaze met his, and her hand stopped inside the paper bag before pulling out the sandwich. "Um... you didn't know? I assumed you were behind her security detail. Then why—"

"I am behind the detail, but she didn't mention that she was getting threats."

The assistant sighed and sat back in her seat.

Laz set his and Journey's lunch on the desk and folded his arms across his chest, trying to remain calm. If he did, Casey would feel comfortable telling him everything she knew. But it was hard not to bolt out of the office space and go in search of his wife.

"I—I shouldn't have said anything. I just assumed...."

"No worries. I'm sure she had a good reason for not telling

me," Laz said, trying to make light of the news but fuming inside.

Lately, things between them had been tense, and considering the arguments they'd been having regarding her work, he could somewhat understand her hesitation. Yet, it bothered him that she didn't trust him enough to know that there was nothing he wouldn't do for her.

Understanding—and seeing to—her safety was his top priority.

Now his mind was reeling, anxious to know what the hell was going on.

"I'm going to go on in," Laz said to Casey and pointed his thumb over his shoulder to Journey's office door.

"Okay. No problem. I'll let her know you're in there. Thanks again for the sandwich. It was right on time."

"Anytime."

Laz strolled into the office and was immediately hit with Journey's signature scent of jasmine permeating the air. He inhaled deeply and released the breath slowly as he glanced around the space.

Not much had changed since he'd been there last, except there were more books, awards, and photos on the floor-to-ceiling shelves lining one side of the room. On the other side were lateral filing cabinets with the bouquet of orchids he had sent her yesterday sitting on top.

He moved further into the space, past two guest chairs, and placed the bag with their lunch on the edge of Journey's large oak desk. He looked around, hoping to spot something that could shed light on what Casey had told him. For the most part, the desk was cleared off except for a couple of pens, an appointment book that was spread open, and a few office supplies. It was as neat and organized as usual. Though tempted, Laz didn't bother tugging on the desk drawers he knew would be locked.

Laz turned to the office door when he heard Journey's voice, and within seconds she walked in, looking as professional and sexy as usual. He always loved seeing her in one of her suits, especially when she was wearing a skirt. She had the prettiest pair of legs he'd ever seen on a woman, and her shoe game was always on point. Those were a few of her features that had initially snagged his attention years ago.

"Hey, you," she said, closing the door behind her.

Laz's first instinct was to lay into her about not telling him about the threats. Instead, he met her in the center of the room and pulled her against him.

"Hey." He lowered his head, and his lips covered hers.

The thought of someone threatening her was still at the forefront of his mind. Yet, as his tongue explored the inner recesses of her luscious mouth, some of the anxiousness seeped from his body, and he put all of his focus on kissing the love of his life.

His right arm tightened around her waist, drawing her closer as he deepened their lip-lock. If only they could stay like that for the rest of their lives. Or hell, he'd even take just staying like that for the rest of the day because then all would be perfect in their lives.

But that wasn't reality, and they definitely needed to talk.

Laz slowly pulled his mouth from hers.

"Wow, what a greeting," Journey said, smiling up at him, her red lipstick slightly smudged. But it didn't detract from her gorgeousness. "Can you be here whenever I return to my office, especially on court days, and kiss me just like that?"

A smile kicked up the corner of Laz's mouth. "Sure. Whatever you want. Whatever you need."

"Hmm...whatever I need...."

Journey laid her head against his chest, careful to stay on his good side, and sighed. Laz knew she was probably tired. The last few days had been like something out of a movie, and though they had lounged around the night before, she hadn't slept well.

"We need to talk," he said before he got too comfortable holding her. He eased his arm from around her waist and perched on the edge of her desk. "Why didn't you tell me that someone's been threatening you? Let me see the letters or whatever the hell they sent. Or was it phone calls that you received?"

She released a heavy sigh. "Laz...please don't—"

"Don't what?" he snapped, unable to help himself but trying to keep his voice down. "Don't protect my wife? Don't find the motherfucker who's sending you threats? Don't what? Why didn't you tell me?"

She huffed out a breath and unlocked her bottom desk drawer. "They were letters. Harmless threats. One of the reasons I didn't say anything was because I didn't want to jeopardize the case. The DA has been on vacation, and if he got wind of the threats, he might pull me from the case."

Laz pushed off the desk, gritting his teeth as he struggled to hold on to his temper. "Jay—"

"Besides, it's not like it's the first time. You know as well as I do that as a lawyer, especially a prosecutor, it comes with a job."

"Let me see the letters—and what's the other reason you didn't tell me?"

"Because...." she started, refusing to make eye contact with him.

That told him what he suspected—that she either thought he didn't care, or she assumed he'd snap and be out for blood. The latter was probably true.

"At the time, we weren't in a good place, and I didn't want to make things worse." She yanked open the drawer and pulled out a manila folder.

She tried to hand the papers to him, but Laz asked, "Are those the originals?"

"No, they're copies," she said, and he accepted them while she stood and moved closer to him. "Prentice has the originals. He had them checked for fingerprints, but there are no clues as to who might've sent them."

Laz set the papers down on the desk and pulled her close. "Look at me," he demanded, and she met his eyes. "You are the most important person in my life. That's never going to change. Whether we are pissed at each other...or on different sides of the world. There is *nothing* that will stop me from loving you and wanting to protect you. Understand?"

Tears filled her eyes, but none fell, and she swallowed hard before giving a slight nod. "Thank you," she whispered.

"You don't have to thank me." He lowered his head and gave her a quick kiss.

They separated, and he picked up the papers, quickly scanning them.

You're wasting your time. Drop the case against Dennis Stratton.

You don't have a case. Drop it. He's innocent!

Drop Stratton's case, Lady ADA. Or else you'll be sorry!

"Now, do you see why I didn't say anything to you? They don't say much, and I didn't really feel threatened. They aren't much different than others I've received over the years."

The words on the pages were typed out in large font and centered on an otherwise blank sheet of the copy paper. Laz was trying not to let the fear of someone threatening his wife show, but it was hard. As a former detective, he knew some threats were harmless, but he'd seen them escalate quickly. And as a husband, it scared him to death that someone could've done something to her, and he struggled to keep his anger at bay.

His concern for Journey's well-being started long before they got together. It was a night he would never forget—the night she was mugged on the way home from work.

When Laz had pulled the man off Journey and started pounding the asshole, he could've easily killed him. She walked away with only bruises, but for months, Laz had always wondered—what if he hadn't been there?

"Are these in the order of the way you received them?" he finally asked.

A frown wrinkled the skin between her eyebrows. "Yeah...I think so. Turn them over; the dates should be on the back of them. Why do you ask?"

"With each one, the threats are escalating."

Journey leaned over him and looked at the papers. "Hmm... I hadn't noticed. That might be why Prentice has hounded me more than once to tell you about this."

"Yeah, this is one time I wished you would've listened to the asshole."

Journey laughed and nudged Laz with her elbow. "Stop it. You two aren't fooling anyone with your mock disdain for each other."

She was right. Prentice was all right with him. He was once a good policeman, and Laz had a lot of respect for the guy. He just didn't like the fact that Prentice got to spend more time with her than he did.

"Until further notice, you don't go anywhere without one of the guys or me. Got that?"

Journey slid her arms around his waist and stared up at him. "I love how protective you are, but can I at least go to the bathroom by myself?" she cracked.

Laz knew she was trying to lighten the mood, and it was damn hard not to relax a little when she was so close and smelled so good. "No. They go where you go," he said seriously.

She laughed and reached up to kiss his lips. "That's where I draw the line, but don't worry. I'll continue to move around town with my shadows. But Laz, I think you might be overreacting."

He shook his head. "Not after someone tried to gun our daughter and me down."

Journey's head snapped up, and her mouth dropped open. "You don't think—"

"Sweetheart, I don't know what to think because I didn't know anything about this," he held up the papers. "But you know me. I don't believe in coincidences.

"Oh, my God. It never crossed my mind that this could be connected to what happened to you, but...." Her words trailed off when her desk phone rang. "I need to get that. The jury might've reached a verdict."

Laz moved away from her desk and released a long breath as she answered the phone. This shit just got real. It was bad enough to come after him, but his wife?

Laz shook his head. He wasn't sure if the two situations were connected, but....

"Who is this?" Journey asked, her voice shaking. "Why do you want the case dropped?"

Laz turned. She was standing behind her desk, gripping the phone tightly with one hand, and her other hand rested on her chest.

Her gaze shot to him, and his heart leaped into his throat at the terror he saw in her eyes. Her face drained of color before she dropped into her seat.

What the hell?

"Who is this?" she said more than once. "Tell me!"

He hurried to her side and snatched the phone from her. "Listen, you sick son of a bitch. Come near her, and I will...." Silence filled the phone line. "Hello? Hello?" Laz yelled.

Journey's horrified eyes stared up at him, and it was like taking a punch to the gut. He set the phone down and gave her his complete attention.

"What did they say, Jay?"

His heart ratcheted up when all she did was stare at him, her eyes wide with fear. Laz cupped her cheek, trying to calm himself in order to get her to relax enough to talk to him.

"Sweetheart, just breathe," he said calmly, breathing in and out slowly until she mirrored his actions. "Now, I need you to tell me what was said."

When she continued looking into his eyes, his heart cracked a little at the defeat he saw in her gaze. "It's all my fault." She bit down on her quivering bottom lip. "I—I'm the reason you and Ari almost died."

Chapter Twenty

Journey's body shook uncontrollably as deep, loud sobs racked her to the core. Tears blinded her eyes and choked her voice with every question Laz asked her. She couldn't stop crying. Each time she tried, a stab of guilt slashed through her, reminding her that she almost lost everything she held dear because of a stupid case.

And for what?

To prove she was the best ADA?

To be the chosen one for the future district attorney position?

None of that was worth almost losing her husband and baby.

Her office door banged open, and she was startled, but Laz tightened his hold around her. She assumed it was Casey, but shame kept her from lifting her head from Laz's chest. That and she physically ached too much to remove her hands from her face.

She hated herself for not having taken the threats seriously.

"What happened?" Casey asked frantically. "Is she okay?"

"Can you hold her calls for a few minutes?" Laz said, and Journey wondered how he could be so calm at the moment. "Unless it's extremely important, she's unavailable. Also, will you grab us a couple of waters?"

"Of course, I'll be right back."

"What's going on?" Angelo's deep voice boomed into the room. Rarely did Journey hear his Spanish accent, but right now, she did.

"She's been getting threats, and it just escalated. Reach out to Wiz. I need the last call she received on her office phone traced."

"Anything else?"

"No, just give us a moment," Laz said, snuggling her closer and placing a kiss on the side of her head.

That only made Journey cry harder. It was the first real cry she had allowed herself since the shooting. Now she didn't think she'd ever be able to pull herself together. She would never be able to forgive herself, knowing that she'd almost gotten Laz and Ari killed.

What if Laz hadn't been as trained and skilled as he was? They could've died out on that street, and it would've been all her fault.

"This isn't your fault," Laz said tenderly, as if reading her mind. "We are going to find this person, and they will regret the day they ever threatened you. I *promise* you that."

Journey soaked up his words, knowing that he never broke his promises. If anyone was going to find the person who had wreaked havoc on their lives, it would be him.

Sniffling, she heaved an exhausted sigh. Her body suddenly felt too heavy to stay upright. All she wanted to do was go somewhere, curl up in a small ball, and never face another soul.

That wasn't realistic.

She needed to pull herself together and help Laz find the bastard who dared to come after them.

Laz eased back and lifted her chin. "I love you," he said with conviction. "This...the call, doesn't change that. Do you understand?"

Journey nodded and eased away from him. She snatched several tissues from the box sitting on the sideboard cabinet behind the desk and dabbed at her eyes. She didn't even want to think about how horrible she probably looked.

"Have a seat," Laz said, moving her office chair closer and holding her elbow while she sat. He propped himself against the desk in front of her. "We're going to get through this."

A soft knock came from the door, and it opened. Journey cringed, not wanting anyone to see her like this. She rested her forehead against Laz. Thankfully, he was blocking her from view.

"Here's the water," Casey said.

"Thanks, you can set them on the edge of the desk," he said while rubbing Journey's back. A few seconds later, the door closed, and quietness filled the room.

Journey didn't move. Neither did Laz. They held their positions until Laz's cell phone vibrated in his pocket. Even then, he didn't make a move—so she didn't either.

She wasn't sure how long they stayed that way until Laz said, "I need you to tell me exactly what they said on the phone."

"I know," she mumbled and eventually lifted her head. Wiping her face was taking energy she didn't have, but she had to pull herself together.

Laz didn't move from in front of her while she jerked open one of her desk drawers. She always kept a makeup kit in her office, just in case. Right now, she was glad she did. Pulling out the pack of makeup remover cloths, a small mirror, and her makeup compact, she quickly fixed her face. There wasn't much she could do about her red eyes, but hopefully, they'd clear up soon.

"Better?" she asked, looking up at Laz.

He smiled, and his gorgeous hazel-green eyes held so much love. What had she ever done to deserve this man?

"You're beautiful. Now, are you ready to get down to business?"

She nodded and thought back to the telephone call. "They said...they said that what happened to my husband was only a warning. I either drop the case or else."

"Or else what?" Laz questioned. "What else did they say?"

"That was it. Hell, that was enough!" She stood abruptly, unable to sit still any longer, and her chair rolled back, bumping into the cabinet.

Her mind raced as she paced the length of her office and back.

Why would someone go to such extremes to force her to drop the case? All that did was make her want to dig deeper and put away everyone involved.

"Was it a man or a woman who called?"

She stopped moving. "I don't know. It was some type of mechanical voice. I couldn't tell; I could barely understand what they were saying."

Journey met Laz's gaze before her eyes went to the black sling holding his arm in place. A cold shiver slid down her spine and seeped into her bones. That shooting could've been so much worse. He could've been killed.

The thought had run through her mind more than once over the last couple of days, but the full force of knowing that it was because of her made her knees buckle. She grabbed onto the back of the guest chair.

"Come on, sit down," Laz said, his hand on her hip, forcing her into the seat.

"Oh, dear God," she murmured more to herself than to him. "You and Ari...could've been killed because of some stupid case!" Journey bit out. Anger suddenly replaced the heartache that swirled inside her, and she banged the side of her fist on her desk. "Some bastard almost took out my family over some stupid case."

"Okay, sweetheart. Let's calm down," Laz said, his voice eerily quiet.

"Calm down? Laz, it's all my fault. Prentice told me I should let you know, but I didn't listen to him."

"I don't always agree with him, but on this, I agree. Don't ever not tell me when someone threatens you."

"I won't, but why aren't you angrier? It's all my fault, Laz."

"No, it's not. I don't blame you for this shit. I blame the motherfucker who set this in motion, and I promise you, we'll get to the bottom of this. At least now we have something we can go on."

"What do you mean?"

"Now I know this is attached to the case you're working on. All we have to do is figure out who's behind this and why."

A knock sounded on the door.

"Come in," Journey said, her voice a little hoarse.

Casey walked in. "I'm sorry to bother you, but the jury has a verdict. It'll be announced in forty-five minutes."

"Okay, thanks. I'll head out shortly.

Casey nodded and backed out of the office, closing the door behind her.

Journey rubbed her eyes. The lack of sleep from the night before was starting to catch up to her. She was pretty sure they'd won the arson murder case, and she should be excited to get to the courthouse to hear the verdict. Yet, her heart was too heavy to care. Right now, all she could think about was the Stratton and Leverage Construction case.

"Laz, I don't know what to do. I can't keep working on this case if it means putting you in danger."

"Don't worry about me. We're going to get this bastard. He should've taken my ass out when he had a chance."

Her head snapped up. "Don't say that."

"We're going to find him or her. The only thing is, you're going to have to be willing to share some information about this case." He slipped his arm around her waist, and pulling her against his hard body, he kissed her. "I know it goes against everything you believe in to share confidential shit, but you might have to, Jay. The team at Supreme and I don't have the same constraints as you, and there's some information we can get faster than you can."

Legal or not, she thought.

Journey bit her bottom lip. There were so many ethical things wrong with what he was implying and proposing. Normally she wouldn't even consider sharing information about the case with an outside source.

But that was before someone tried to take out her family.

"Where do we start?"

Chapter Twenty-One

"You never cease to impress me, counselor," Parker said as he and Angelo escorted Journey out of the courtroom. "First with the closing arguments earlier today, and now with the win. If I ever need a lawyer, I want you on my team."

"Thanks," she said, giving him a slight smile as they entered the busier-than-usual hallway. "It was a tough one, but justice prevailed. And hopefully, you'll never need a lawyer, but if you do, I'll be there."

Despite being exhausted and operating on fumes, Journey was happy that she'd won the arson murder case. She and her team had worked on it for six months, and nothing about it had been easy. During the investigation, there were times when she didn't think she could build a solid case. There had been twists, turns, and even a couple of setbacks. In the end, she managed to convince the jury that the defendant was responsible for the fire to the warehouse and the death of the homeless man found inside.

Journey strolled down the hallway with Parker and Angelo

on either side of her. She might've given Laz a hard time when he originally insisted on details, but not anymore. Not after that phone call this afternoon that shook her to the soles of her feet. It was scary as hell knowing that someone was out there watching her and her family.

Still, she had second thoughts about pulling Laz and his team in on the case against Dennis Stratton, but this was a special circumstance. Tonight, instead of going home after work, she and Prentice would head over to Supreme Security. Hopefully, together, they all could get to the bottom of why someone was willing to kill to keep this case from going to trial.

"Do you need to stop anywhere before we take you to Supreme?" Angelo asked as they moved through the crowded hallway.

"Yeah, I'm not scheduled to be there until eight. I need to stop back at the office, and I want to go home to change clothes." She could also use a drink to take the edge off an emotional day, but she kept that thought to herself.

Without missing a step, Angelo dug into the inside pocket of his suit jacket and pulled out his buzzing cell phone.

"Yeah," he answered, then slowed and put his arm out for Journey and Parker to stop. "Will do."

"What's up?" Parker asked before Journey could get the words out.

"Myles said the media has the front of the courthouse in chaos, but he's not sure why. He'll meet us at the side entrance."

They headed to the entrance that Journey often used. The moment Angelo pushed open the door, cameras flashed, and members of the media rushed toward them. Parker cursed under his breath as he and Angelo flanked her, moving in perfect precision to block anyone from getting close.

"ADA Dimas, is it true your husband, a former cop, was gunned down the other day?"

"How is your husband? Is it true he was a crooked cop?"

"Is it true your husband and daughter were almost killed the other day?"

Fear and anger warred inside of Journey with each question thrown at her. Laz had told her that Hamilton had been able to keep the information about the shooting out of the media. Apparently, they'd somehow gotten wind of it.

"Did the shooting have anything to do with one of your cases?" a reporter shouted.

"Is it true that city councilwoman Tamar Warner has been accepting bribes from Leverage Construction and possibly other companies?" another reporter asked.

Shock blasted through Journey, and her steps faltered.

How the....

"Keep moving," Angelo whispered close to Journey's ear.

He had a hand at the small of her back while shielding their faces from camera flashes. All Journey could think about was that either Prentice told someone about what they'd learned, or Marta talked to someone. Her guess was the latter. She trusted Prentice with her life, and he knew how important this case was to her.

"ADA Dimas, why do you have a security detail? Does it have anything to do with your husband being shot at?"

Journey was bombarded with questions, and anxiousness blasted through her in the midst of the chaos. Her mind reeled with each one, and if she had any doubts about meeting with Supreme Security, they were erased at that moment. They had to get to the bottom of whatever was going on.

"Myles is on the left," Parker said only loud enough for her to hear.

Journey assumed Angelo saw him since he was already

moving them in that direction. The small crowd followed close behind, still lobbing questions at her.

Shielding her with his body and pushing a cameraman back, Parker yanked open the back door to the SUV. "Get in, slide over, and put your head down." Journey did as he said, and Parker was barely in the car next to her before Myles started driving. She didn't lift her head, especially since someone was knocking on the back door window with questions.

Myles laid on the horn and kept inching forward.

"Dammit, get the hell out of the way!" Angelo yelled from the passenger seat. "Now, if we ran over one of them, they'd be claiming that we were the ones in the wrong," he mumbled and put his cell phone to his ear.

A few minutes later, the vehicle sped up.

"Okay, you can sit up," Parker said. "Are you okay?"

Journey slowly lifted her head, then blew out an irritated breath. "Yeah, I'm all right. Just mad as hell." And tired, hungry, frustrated...and the list went on and on.

She was also scared that this was just the beginning.

"Yeah, she's fine," Journey heard Angelo say. "Damn, man, chill. I told you she's fine. What? You think we can't do our jobs?" Though his voice was raised, there was humor in his tone, and Journey assumed he was talking to Laz.

"How you guys do this every day all day is a mystery to me," she said to Parker as she dug in the side pocket of her laptop bag for her cell phone. It was clear they were well trained. They'd shielded her and got her into the truck without being trampled by the mob, and they didn't seem shaken at all.

Parker chuckled. "All in a day's work."

Journey glanced at her phone screen and saw that she had a couple of text messages. Instead of reading them, she pulled up

Prentice's contact information. She needed to talk to him before doing anything else.

"Hello," Prentice said when he answered the phone.

"Hey, it's me. Please tell me that you didn't tell anyone about Tamar," Journey said quietly, but at the moment, she didn't care if the guys in the truck were listening. She wanted to know how the media found out about the claims against Tamar.

"Not a word, but I'm going to find out who did," he said with conviction. "We still on to meet at Supreme?" he asked.

Journey confirmed and filled him in on the latest, including being ambushed by the media. When she was finished her recap and gave him instructions on the next steps, she huffed out an exhausted breath.

I just need this day to be over.

Chapter Twenty-Two

An hour later, Journey walked into Supreme Security, and Laz was the first person she saw. He was waiting in the back foyer, and the tenderness in his pretty eyes made her heart turn over in her chest. His hair was pulled into a ponytail at his nape, and he was finally getting some color back in his skin. She hadn't seen him look this healthy in days.

Her gaze took in the rest of him. Whether in a black suit, his usual uniform, or jeans and a Henley like he was currently wearing, the man was *fine* and a sight for tired eyes.

It didn't matter that she'd seen him earlier. All she wanted to do was be wrapped in his strong arms and forget about her drama-filled day. Usually, she wasn't so needy, but right now, she wanted him to hold her. To remind her that as long as they had each other, they could get through anything. Because the last few days of her rollercoaster ride of emotions were starting to wear on her.

As she hurried to him, Laz didn't say a word. He opened his arm to her, and she molded her body against his. Like him, she couldn't wait until he could get rid of the sling. A one-armed hug was okay, but it was nothing compared to the feel of both of his strong arms embracing her tightly.

"What a day," she said, her cheek resting against his broad chest. "I can't wait until it's over. That way, I can start anew in the morning with no drama."

Laz's hearty chuckle vibrated against her ear, bringing a smile to her face.

"Yeah, let's hope." He kissed the top of her head. "How about a drink and a little dinner before we start tackling the *drama* that is our life?"

She leaned back and smiled at him. "If 'by drink' you mean a shot of tequila or whisky, then I'd say that sounds heavenly. I also wouldn't turn down food." Especially since she'd only had a few bites of her sandwich at lunch before having to rush back to court.

Laz led her upstairs to a meeting space with several long tables with comfortable-looking chairs, a screen that came out of the ceiling and was as wide as one of the walls. They called it the war room. It was where they usually met up as a group to discuss significant assignments and debrief. The space could easily hold fifty people or more, but tonight there would only be a handful of them trying to determine who was threatening her.

"Come on in. The food table is set up in the back," Laz said, his arm around her waist.

The moment Journey stepped further into the space, the enticing scent of oregano and other spices met her nose. She set her laptop bag on one of the tables and followed Laz to the mini buffet. Her mouth watered when she saw the pan of lasagna, salad, a vegetable tray, bread sticks, and a few more side dishes. It looked like others had already eaten, but there was still plenty of food left. There were also bottles of liquor, soda, and tea at the far end of the table.

While she fixed a plate for her and Laz, he poured her a two-finger glass of whiskey and grabbed a couple bottles of water.

"Where is everyone else?" Journey asked when they sat down to eat.

"They've already started working on the situation and will be here in a minute. I know you're concerned about confidentiality, but Jay, I hope you know that you can trust all of the guys. What's discussed in this room will stay in here."

"I know."

"There's something I did find out," Laz said, wiping his mouth with a linen napkin. "The gun used to shoot me was the same one used to shoot your witness, Fred Jacobs."

An involuntary shiver rocked Journey. Laz was always so cavalier about guns, shootings, and death, and she knew it had a lot to do with him being former law enforcement. But for her, it all was very disturbing, especially when the person shot was her husband.

She lifted the glass of whiskey, slammed it back, and grimaced, with her eyes tightly closed, at the burn that slid down the back of her throat.

Goodness. Whew, that's strong.

She blinked several times. She could already feel the liquor flowing through her body and giving her that extra little something to get her through the evening. Everything around her seemed brighter and clearer.

When she glanced up, Laz was smiling at her. "Would you like another?

"Uh, no. I think I'm good." She cleared her throat and blinked a few more times. "How'd they find the shooter?" She was getting ready to eat a forkful of lasagna but stopped when she recognized the expression on Laz's face.

Setting her fork down, she braced herself. "What did you do?"

"I didn't break any laws," he hurried to say. "Well, not many, but don't worry. I didn't mess up Ted's case. It's solid, and the shooters are going away for a *very* long time."

"Yeah, tell it to the prosecutor, who'll be asking questions about how the evidence was obtained."

A slow smile kicked up the corners of Laz's tempting lips. "That's not going to be a problem. The case will be solid because, for years, the world's greatest prosecutor has practically beat the law into me. I know it like the back of my hand."

Despite her concern, Journey laughed. "Flattery will get you nowhere."

He chuckled and wiped his mouth with a napkin before turning serious. "Trust me, sweetheart, everything is covered. The shooters gave their statement admitting to their part, and they've been cooperative."

Journey nodded. She could only imagine what Laz had done to get them to admit to murder and attempted murder. Actually, she didn't want to know. As long as he didn't end up in jail—or worse—she was just glad he had found the shooters.

"I'm assuming no one admitted to the threats."

He shook his head and drank almost half of his bottled water. "No, and what I learned a few minutes ago, someone gave them the gun to do the hit. They don't know who hired them or what they look like."

Journey sighed and sat back in her chair. "It's unbelievable what people will do for money, and to accept it without question is just stupid."

Laz shrugged, but before he could respond, some of the guys strolled in. Ashton and Hamilton were the only ones she hadn't seen today. They greeted her with hugs before making a beeline to the food.

Laz had mentioned that the guys had eaten, but apparently, it hadn't been the ones in the room. Their plates were piled high as if they hadn't eaten in days.

"I'm sorry about the ambush at the courthouse, Jay," Hamilton said when he sat across from her with his plate of food. "And Laz, I put a call in to the person who told me they'd keep a lid on that situation. Needless to say, they were surprised and said that they would research the situation. They'll get back to me."

"Thanks, man," Laz said. "I knew the media would get wind of it at some point. I had hoped it would be after we found out who was behind it."

"We'll find them," Ashton said, sitting next to Journey. "Thanks for trusting us enough to bring us in on your case... well, at least the part regarding the threat to you and Laz."

Journey should be thanking them. All of them were former detectives, except for Parker, who was former SWAT. They all were the best of the best at their jobs. She had no doubt that together they would find the person who was after her and who had tried taking out her husband.

"I appreciate you all for stepping up to help," she said. "I won't be able to give you everything about the case related to Dennis Stratton, but I'll share what I can. I think the threats have something to do with someone connected to either the merger or the city contract that the company was awarded recently."

"Egypt did some research on the merger that fell through," Parker said.

He sat to Laz's left with two plates of food and a beer in front of him. It never ceased to amaze her how much he ate, despite having no fat anywhere on his muscular body.

"Leverage Construction was in negotiations with the Brockman Group, but we learned from a former Brockman employee that the owner didn't get along with Dennis Stratton. According to the woman, the company pulled out of the deal after the valuation analysis proved the company wasn't worth as much as Stratton claimed it was."

Journey had figured as much after the conversation with Marta. "That leads me to think that the threats aren't from someone involved with the merger. I'm thinking we focus on employees and the contract," she said. "Especially since the city just decided to put the project on hold until further notice."

"Hmm...when did that happen?" Laz asked.

"I found out this afternoon, but I'm not sure when the news will be made public."

Laz nodded. "Which means a stakeholder, subcontractor, or whoever else was listed in the proposal is going to be seriously pissed that the deal is on hold," he said as he gently massaged the back of Journey's neck. His touch felt so good that she had to keep herself from moaning.

"Good point. The threat was to drop Stratton's case so that it wouldn't go to trial, which would've kept the city from putting the multimillion-dollar contract on hold," Ashton said. "People do crazy things they wouldn't normally do when money is at stake."

"Since the threats didn't work and money won't be exchanging hands, someone might be mad enough to actually come after you personally," Laz added, looking at her with concern.

"They already did that when they attacked you," Journey said quietly, sadness and a twinge of guilt creeping through her. There was nothing more personal than hurting her family.

Laz pulled her close and placed a kiss against her temple. "I'm talking about *you*. Someone might try to hurt you physically. We're going to have your back, but Jay, you're going to have to be diligent about your safety, too."

Journey nodded in agreement. She and Laz had already agreed that she would stay the course with the case and not transfer it to someone else. Part of her felt secure knowing that he and the guys would be looking after her. The other part of her wouldn't breathe normally until the person coming for her was caught.

"I will, and you guys are right about us starting with the contractors listed in Leverage Construction's initial proposal," she said, pulling the thick document out of her laptop bag. "I haven't had a chance to dive into what they submitted to the city yet, and I'm in court much of the day tomorrow. It might be a day or two before I can take my time and go through every page."

"One of us can do that," Laz volunteered and agreed to make a copy of the document before they left. "We'll check out every subcontractor, individual, or business they might've listed."

The longer they brainstormed and divided up tasks, the more Journey appreciated their help. She kept telling herself that she wasn't breaking any laws or jeopardizing any confidentiality aspects of the case. The thing that made her feel okay about going this route with their task force-like setup was that, together, they'd find the person angry enough to put a hit out on Laz.

The DA's office could handle everything Supreme's team was willing to do but not as quickly. For Laz and his coworkers, there was no red tape, no signatures of approval needed, and they could do most things under the radar.

Journey was actually a little jealous of the agency's freedom, especially since the DA's office was always under a microscope. They had to operate by the book, and even then, their motives were questioned by individuals and the government.

A knock sounded on the door, and they all turned toward it as Prentice walked in with a manilla file folder.

"Well, look who decided to make an appearance. The all-mighty Prentice Johnson, investigator of all investigators," Laz cracked, and Journey elbowed him.

"Whatever, *Lazarus,*" Prentice said with mock disdain, getting a few chuckles from the guys around the table. "I'm too tired and hungry to verbally spar with you tonight."

Journey didn't know what it was with them two. It was as if they got a thrill from throwing potshots at each other.

"Good to see you, Prentice. Help yourself to the food over there," Hamilton said.

"Thanks, man, and hey, everybody. Sorry I'm late. I had to follow up on some information I received just before leaving the office," he said as he fixed a plate. "Journey, I was able to hunt down Shawn Ridley."

"Who is he?" Laz asked.

"He was an accountant at Leverage until a few months ago when he quit," Journey explained. "What did he have to say?"

"Pretty much what Marta told us. The company was being mismanaged, and Stratton demanded they handle the accounting as he saw fit. Shawn said that it got to be too much, and he quit. And he's the one who leaked the information about Tamar taking bribes."

Journey frowned, wondering what he had to gain by sharing that information. "Did he say why, and why now?"

"According to him, he didn't say anything sooner because he didn't want to get the other accountants, Marta and Joyce, into trouble. But after hearing about Joyce's death, he knew the company would be investigated, and he couldn't keep quiet any longer. I got a formal statement from him, and he's willing to testify to everything he told me."

"Good," Journey said with a yawn. They'd been in the

meeting a couple of hours now, and she was more than ready to go home and curl up with her husband.

"He also confirmed that Stratton was paying Councilwoman Warner," Prentice continued. "But he doesn't have any physical proof.

"That's okay. Our office will start digging into Tamar Warner's dealings. If she's guilty of the claims against her, she might also be the one behind the threats. With Stratton in jail, possibly for the rest of his life, that would stop whatever monies she was receiving from him," Journey said.

"You think she's capable of killing someone or hiring someone to kill?" Laz asked. He knew of the woman and Journey's prickly relationship with her, but he didn't know her personally.

Journey thought about the question before saying, "I honestly don't know. I can't see her stooping to that level, but I also never thought she'd take bribes. So..." she shrugged, "...my team and I will research everything there is to know about the woman. From her finances to her personal life, we won't stop until we know everything."

"Jay, I'm not sure if you know, but she's been recently seen around town with Tony Price," Ashton said. "We have photos, and in recent, I mean the last few months."

"Yeah, I know. I saw them at Double Trouble a few days ago, and Tony mentioned that their relationship was new," Journey said.

"You didn't mention that you saw him lately," Laz said. He didn't sound mad or jealous, only surprised.

"I didn't think about it." But now that his name was brought up, maybe she should call and ask him some questions. She wasn't sure how to do that without raising suspicion in case he didn't know what his girlfriend was up to.

First, I should determine if she is actually taking bribes, Journey thought.

The door burst open, and Journey was startled when Mason stormed in.

Like the others in the room, he was over six feet tall, broad, and probably could easily bench-press five hundred pounds. Bald with dark skin and a set of magnetic eyes that were hard to look away from, he was the embodiment of a fearless leader. His no-nonsense demeanor demanded respect, and right now, he looked as if he was ready to strangle someone.

"You two, in my office now!" he roared, pointing at Parker and then Laz before marching back out the door.

Parker groaned, and Laz sighed before they both stood. Clearly, they knew what was going on even if Journey didn't.

"What did you do?" she asked under her breath, worried that he had really screwed up this time.

He gave her a cocky grin before placing a quick kiss on her lips. "Nothing. I'll be back in a minute." He walked out as if he didn't have a worry in the world.

Now she was the one sighing. "Do either of you know what that was all about?" she asked the other guys in the room.

"Nope," Hamilton and Ashton said simultaneously, and she knew they were lying. But like Laz and Parker, they didn't seem too concerned.

Journey wasn't sure what was going on, but she hoped Laz hadn't done anything stupid to get himself fired. One of them needed to have money coming in.

After today, she was seriously thinking about quitting her job very soon.

Chapter Twenty-Three

Mason was standing behind his large desk when Parker and Laz finally strolled in. They closed the door and moved closer; he wanted to strangle them for different reasons. One was good at putting his life in danger without thinking. The other didn't know yet, but his life very well might be in danger.

"What's up, boss?" Parker asked, leaning on the back of the chair in front of the desk.

"I told you two to stand down and let the cops handle the shooting." He looked pointedly at Laz, knowing he was the one to pull Parker in. "But then I find out that, not only did you not listen, but you put three guys in the hospital. What part of *stand down* didn't you understand?"

The guy might be a heartbeat away from crazy, but he was one of the best security specialists Mason had ever worked with. Still, he was a pain in the ass most days, even if his instincts were always on point.

Laz cleared his throat and moved forward. "Come on,

Mase. Parker is innocent. This is all on me, and I take full responsibility."

"Good, because you're suspended for thirty days."

"Wait! What?" Laz's hazel-green eyes sparked.

"Did I stutter?" Mason couldn't be mad about Laz's actions, because had it been him and someone gunned him down, he would've responded the same way. When he ordered Laz to let the cops handle the situation, he had known that Laz wouldn't. It wasn't in his nature to sit back and let someone else take over.

But Mason prided himself on taking care of his people—protecting them at all cost. It was his duty to watch over Laz since the jerk didn't have the good sense to look out for himself. The man thought he was invincible. A thirty-day suspension was the only way Mason could get him to sit his ass down somewhere and let that shoulder heal.

When Laz started to speak, Mason lifted his hand. "It's a paid suspension, and you already know that we will find whoever has targeted your family. In the meantime, I don't want to see you here for *any* reason. Not to use the gym, not to meet any of the guys here for lunch, and I sure as hell don't want to hear that you're using one of the crash rooms. Get your ass out of my office, and go home!"

"Seriously, Mase?" Laz ground out. "I have to—"

"The only thing you have to do is go home and take care of yourself, Laz. I need you to heal so that you can get back on the job. No one needs you running around beating up on thugs and helping the cops do *their* job. We got you."

"You know I can't sit this out," Laz said and dropped into one of the chairs.

"The guys and I will work with Journey. We're going to find the asshole who is behind all of this."

Laz sighed loudly. "Well, don't punish Parker. I blackmailed him into going with me that night."

Parker snorted, and Mason glared at the younger man. He was pretty sure there had been no blackmailing going on, but he'd play along.

"It doesn't matter. I'm benching both of you," Mason said. "When I give an order, I expect it to be followed. Besides, what were you two thinking going after those guys? I pay you to protect folks, not go around beating the crap out of people."

There was no doubt in his mind that they both could handle themselves, and he was glad they got the shooters. Still, the situation could've easily gotten out of hand with both of them getting hurt—or worse.

Besides, there were other reasons he was benching Parker.

"Laz, you can leave. Parker, you stay."

"I'm sorry, man," Laz said, standing and giving Parker a fist bump. "I owe you one."

"Yes, you do," Parker smirked. "And I plan to collect."

When Laz left, closing the door behind him, Parker turned to Mason. "So, what's really going on?"

"You're going to have to lay low for a while," Mason said, and woke up his laptop.

"Okaaaaay," Parker said slowly. "What happened?"

Mason turned his laptop around so Parker could see the photo that showed up on national news and the internet.

"Aw, hell," Parker growled. He turned and punched the air before linking his fingers behind his head. "I wasn't thinking. Damn, I should've been more careful."

One of the cameramen outside the courthouse had managed to get a photo of Journey, and Parker was partially in the frame. His head was slightly turned, but despite the cosmetic surgery he'd undergone years ago, anyone who knew him before then might still be able to tell it was him.

"I'm sorry, man," Mason said. "Had I known Journey would be bombarded by the press, there's no way I would've let you be on her detail. We should've known that this could happen one day."

"No apology necessary. If it weren't for you giving me a chance at a normal life, I don't know what I would've done. Hell, I don't even know if I'd still be alive. I'll lay low, but if my father or his people happen to see that photo, it won't take long for them to find out who I work for or where."

"Yeah, we'll cross that bridge when we get to it, but your dad doesn't want to go to war with us. Because that's exactly what will happen if he or his goons come knocking. You're family, and we take care of family."

They shook hands and pulled each other in for a one-armed hug. "I appreciate that. What do you want me to do? Leave town? Leave the country?"

Mason had been thinking about that for the last few minutes. "No, I want you to stay close so we can have your back. You can work the front desk for a few weeks...or months. Who knows, maybe we'll get lucky, and your father and his people will still believe that you're dead."

Chapter Twenty-Four

It had been four days since the meeting at Supreme Security and four days of still not knowing for sure who was behind the threats. Laz was trying to focus on the here and now, but his mind kept wandering.

Usually, he looked forward to the *Save Our Boys* annual fundraiser. It was a great cause, and the organization had helped tens of thousands of young men reach their full potential. But tonight, as he stood at the bar with Hamilton and Kenton in a spectacularly decorated ballroom, it was hard to totally enjoy the evening. There was still someone out there who was a threat to his family.

He had finally told Ted about the threats and handed over everything they'd learned about the situation, including the information Journey and her team dug up on Councilwoman Tamar Warner. The woman had started from humble beginnings but worked her way through college and law school.

They learned that in the last three years, Tamar's income had doubled. It looked like she was putting her law degree to use. In addition to being a city councilwoman, she made money consulting for nonprofits. Recently, she'd started spending more money than it appeared she made by buying expensive real estate, cars, and taking luxurious trips.

She was definitely a person of interest when it came to threatening Journey and targeting him. The problem was, she was nowhere to be found. Law enforcement had issued an APB —all-points bulletin—but so far, no one had seen her. There had also been no more threats to Journey.

Still, Laz had suggested they lay low and skip the event. He wasn't one for hiding out, but when it came to Journey's safety, he didn't like taking risks. But considering how sexy she looked in the yellow—or as she referred to the color, *daffodil*—dress, he liked the idea of showing her off.

She was standing near their table with Dakota and Zenobia. There might've been beautiful women in attendance and dressed to impress, but none were as gorgeous as his woman.

The evening gown flowed over Journey's fit body like liquid gold. Laz wasn't sure when she had purchased the dress, but he was glad she had. The silky, halter-necked garment crisscrossed over her full breasts, and the wide straps hung down the middle of her bare back.

Besides the dynamic color and the way it draped over her curvy body, what really sold the outfit was the crazy-high split that went up past her thigh. Her long shapely leg was on full display, along with a pair of sexy-ass rhinestone shoes. The heels were at least four inches tall, with an ankle strap that enhanced her sexiness.

"I'll be back," Laz said to the guys. Several of his friends were in attendance, not only because they usually supported the organization but also because Laz still wanted someone watching his and Journey's back.

Usually, Supreme Security was the contracted security firm for the event, but this year, the organizers had gone with another company, which surprised Laz. He'd been active with the organization for years, and in doing so, the organizers always used Supreme. Not this year, though, supposedly because of budget cuts. There were only a couple of security guards present.

Journey smiled when she noticed Laz approaching, and it seemed like the whole room brightened. He was one lucky bastard, and each day he spent with her made him much more grateful.

"Hey there," she said.

"Hey, yourself, beautiful." Laz placed a kiss against her lips, not caring if some of her lipstick came off. "I just wanted to come over and see how you were doing."

She grinned at him. "That should be my line, considering you're still banged up. No pun intended."

Laz laughed. A week ago, he couldn't laugh at the situation, but a lot had happened in the past week. They still hadn't gotten the person behind the hit on him, but at least they'd gotten the shooters off the street and Nazir's murderer.

And Laz and Journey's relationship was stronger than it had been in a long time. They still had no answers regarding the next steps with Journey's career, but he had no doubt they'd figure it out. They had to because he was never walking away from her, and he'd fight like hell to keep her from ever leaving him.

She straightened his bowtie. "I should've known you would ditch your tuxedo jacket," she said. "Actually, I thought the tie would've been gone by now, too."

Laz smiled at her. "I kept the tie on for you. I know how much you like it," he crooned and leaned in to nuzzle her neck, just behind her ear. It was bad enough that he had to wear a suit for work. Having to wear one tonight was a pain, especially with the damn sling. He had rid himself of the jacket a few minutes ago, leaving him in a crisp white shirt and black tuxedo pants.

"Well, you still look extremely handsome. I can't wait to get to our room where I can strip you out of your clothes," she said, a sensual sparkle in her eyes and a sinister smirk on her red lips.

Laz laughed. "You got everyone believing you're this sweet little prosecutor when actually, you're a vixen in sheep's clothing. Well, except for tonight. Tonight, you could give a dominatrix a run for her money. Baby, you look amazing in this dress, and I can't wait to get you out of it. How about we write the organization a fat check and get out of here?"

It was nice that the fundraiser was being held in a luxury hotel. They booked a suite for two nights, agreeing that they needed a little R&R. Now, all Laz wanted to do was carry her upstairs and make good use of their room.

"You, my love, are such a sweet talker, but we're not going anywhere yet. Besides, Zen is going to be singing soon. I've missed enough over the last few months. I don't want to miss her performance."

Laz huffed out a mock irritated breath. "Fine. We can stay, but when we leave here, you're all mine."

"I'm all yours now and forever," she whispered and cupped his cheek. Brushing her thumb gently over his light stubble, she flashed that grin again. "But when we get upstairs, I'll let you do whatever you want to me."

Laz lowered his head until his mouth covered hers. The kiss started out soft and sweet but quickly turned passionate. God, he loved this woman, and kissing her was definitely his favorite thing in the world to do.

"All right, you two, knock it off," Dakota said from behind Laz and swatted his back. "Journey, we're heading back to the buffet. Find us when you finish smooching with the one-armed man."

Laz couldn't help but laugh when he lifted his head. "You're lucky you're like a sister to me," he said to Dakota as she walked away snickering.

"I'm going to go and get some more food. Do you want anything?" Journey asked.

"Maybe another slice of prime rib."

"You got it. Oh, and have you seen Tony yet?" Journey asked Laz.

Laz frowned. "Since when am I supposed to keep up with your knuckleheaded ex-boyfriend?"

"Laz." She smacked her lips, and her perfectly arched eyebrows bunched together. "Why do you always have to call him names?"

"Seriously? I can't be nice to the guy. He's your ex, Jay. I'm supposed to be all brooding and jealous when he's around or when you talk about him."

She shook her head. "You're too much."

"Besides, he *is* a knucklehead if he let you go. Actually, he's a damn idiot," Laz amended, but he was glad the jerk walked away from her. That gave him the opportunity to have her for himself.

"It wasn't like that, and you know it," Journey defended weakly.

It was definitely like that, but Laz had no intentions of debating with her. Tony had been crazy in love with her and wanted to marry her. Thankfully, Journey hadn't felt the same. Instead of continuing to date her hoping that she'd change her mind, he moved on.

"So, I'll take that as a—you haven't seen him," she said with a laugh while adjusting his bowtie again. He was starting to think she had a thing for bowties. "I wanted to give him a heads-up about his girlfriend without sharing any details. I don't want him to get tangled up in her mess once the Feds find her."

Journey had been working day and night the last couple of days, and she gathered enough proof to implicate Tamar Warner.

"He might already be, and it might be too late. I'm sure he's already been questioned about her whereabouts. Anyway, why do you care?"

"I care because he and I might not be together, but I still consider him a friend."

"Well, just make sure he's a distant friend. I don't want him thinking he has any chance with you now that his woman is going to jail."

"Aww, there's my caveman." Journey slipped her arms around his neck. "For a minute there, I didn't think your jealous streak would show. I guess I should feel flattered."

"You know, if you kiss me, that'll help me feel more secure in our relationship. It'll remind me that I have nothing to worry about when it comes to you two."

She kissed him sweetly, and when he tried to deepen their lip-lock, she pressed her hands against his chest and eased away from him.

"There will be more of that later. Right now, try to be good while I.... Oh, there's the DA and his wife. I'll see you in a few."

Laz shook his head as she took off across the large banquet room. He gave her one last glance before heading to the buffet. Clearly, he was going to have to get his own prime rib.

At least his wife was happy and having a good time. Once they got through this mess circling her case, they could focus on having more fun evenings. That was something he was looking forward to.

* * *

Journey finally headed in the direction of the buffet. After speaking with her boss and his wife, she ran into a former coworker. She'd been working so much that she didn't realize just how much she missed socializing outside of the office. It felt good to be out mingling.

"Wow, you look incredible."

Journey whirled around, almost tripping over her feet, when she recognized Tony's voice. "Why, thank you," she said with her best English accent, then giggled. "I've been looking for you all night. I was starting to think you weren't coming. Where have you been hiding?" she joked.

"Nowhere. I've been around, trying to get everyone to dig a little deeper into their pockets and purses and donate more money," he said, smiling down at her. "I've been wanting to talk to you about something. Walk with me. We can talk while I go and check on the silent auction. The bids have exceeded last year's total, but I'm hoping I can nudge people to bid a little higher on a couple of items."

Journey glanced over her shoulder but didn't see Laz. She also didn't see Hamilton and Kenton. They were all probably together somewhere. She was hesitant to leave and go to the ballroom next door, where the items for the auction were set up.

"Come on. I'll bring you back before your husband sends out a search party."

Journey laughed and walked out with him. "Ahh, you know him well. Okay, but only for a minute. I wanted to talk to you, too...about Tamar. I saw photos of you guys, and you looked really happy with her. I'm not sure if you know—"

"Don't tell me you believe the lies about her accepting bribes," Tony said, getting a little defensive. "They are lies, Journey, and I'm sure her lawyers will prove it."

"For your sake, I hope you're right. I still care about you. I don't want you to get hurt if everything is true about her. You don't happen to know where she is, do you?"

He didn't speak for a moment, and before they reached the area where the silent auction was, he slowed.

"Listen. I'm only going to say...." Loud laughter drowned out whatever he was going to say. "Let's go over there so I can at least hear myself."

Journey followed him to a secluded hallway only a few steps away from the auction room. They moved to a quiet corner, and he stood in front of her, blocking the view of others.

"Okay, let me say this, and I'm only going to say it once." His voice was low, and there was a bit of harshness in his tone. "You should've dropped the case."

Journey leaned back and frowned. "What? Why would I do that? If your woman is doing what she's being accused of doing, she deserves to spend time behind bars. Don't let her good looks and sweet-talking blind you to the truth, Tony. She's in serious trouble."

Journey didn't mean to come off so strong, but how dare he tell her that she should've dropped the case. He should know....

Her thoughts screeched to a halt. "What did you say to me?" she asked and glanced uneasily around, hoping someone would walk down that particular hallway. Or at least walk past it.

"You heard me," Tony said, his low voice a near-snarl. "If you would've just dropped the case, none of this would be happening. You've ruined everything. It was bad enough that you dumped me and married someone else, but this...."

He balled his fist and gritted his teeth as if struggling to keep his composure.

"By working with Dennis Stratton, I finally would have had a chance to take my business to the next level. I needed that city contract we were collaborating on, but you just had to have him arrested."

Journey's mouth gaped. "Are you kidding me? The guy murdered his employee. What would you have me do? Let him walk around town as if he hadn't done anything?"

"I needed that money! My employees were counting on me," he said as if she hadn't just spoken. His words held more anguish than anger. "And then I met the woman of my dreams, and you ruined that, too. She left me so that she could hide out God knows where!" he snapped, his face only inches from hers.

"Back up!" Journey snapped.

He didn't move.

"I said back the hell off of me!" She pushed against his chest, surprised at how solid he was. He'd clearly been working out. When he still didn't move, panic inched through her.

"You and I could've been so good together. Instead, you decided to marry that white guy when you told me you never wanted marriage. I guess I wasn't the right color for you, huh."

Anger surged to the surface, overriding her panic. "Be careful, Tony. You keep talking, and you're going to say something you'll regret."

He chuckled. "I doubt that. What the hell do you think you can do to me?"

She opened her mouth to scream but gasped instead when she felt the gun in her side.

"Let's move," he said, grabbing her upper arm with his other hand.

"No!" Journey dug in her heels as best she could in her stilettos, but he was still able to drag her along.

She couldn't go with him.

She couldn't leave that area.

She had to do something, but with the barrel of a gun jammed into her ribs, she felt helpless.

"Tony, think about what you're doing. Let go of me. You're never going to get away with this."

"Oh, you would be surprised at what I've gotten away with. Since you didn't drop the case when you were warned, there's only one other thing to do. Kill you."

Chapter Twenty-Five

Laz's cell phone vibrated, and he leaned back slightly in the chair and dug it out of the front of his pocket. Ashton's name flashed across the screen.

"What's up, man?" Laz asked. Standing with the phone pressed to his ear, he headed to the ballroom door to hear better. As he moved between tables and people huddling together and talking, he looked around the huge room for Journey.

Where the hell is she? The last time I saw her, she was talking to some woman.

"A couple of things," Ashton said, cutting into Laz's thoughts. "First, your boy Remy is the one who leaked the info about the shooting."

"That asshole," Laz mumbled. "I shouldn't be surprised. If he could, he'd probably kill me himself."

"In his defense, it wasn't intentional. I found footage of him talking to a reporter about some other shootings in that area. The reporter said something about cops not being around when needed, and Remy disagreed. Then he said it was a tough area where even detectives get gunned down. He caught himself, stopped talking, but then kept going. He didn't mention your name, but—"

"A good reporter could research from there," Laz finished.

"Exactly. Are you still at the fundraiser?" Ashton asked.

"Yeah, why? You decided to attend?"

"No, but I have some information. I figured I'd share it with you before pulling Ted in on it. We've ID'd a person of interest who might be behind the shooting."

Laz's heart stopped. "Who?"

"It's a long shot, but I think Tony could be involved."

"Tony who?" Laz asked, quickly going through his mental rolodex. "Do you know how many Tonys I...." his voice trailed off, and his heart stuttered. His gaze roamed around the ballroom again, and he moved around the perimeter of the space, determined to find his wife. "Please tell me it's not—"

"Tony Price. Journey's ex. His computer business is listed as one of the subcontractors in the city housing contract. He does more than just repair computers at his tech company. Had the contract not been put on hold, he would've been hired to install smart home technology into some of the houses. The budget for his part was almost one mil."

Damn. Damn. Damn.

"Wiz pulled Tony's financials," Ashton continued, "and Price is on the verge of bankruptcy. The contract would've been just what he needed to get his business out of the red. But with the contract going away—"

"His business will tank," Laz said absently while he continued glancing around.

Seemed like even more people had arrived, making it harder to find Journey. She wasn't supposed to leave his sight.

"Ash, keep digging. Let's make sure it's him before we

notify Ted, assuming he doesn't already have Tony on his radar."

Laz disconnected the call, and his gut churned with worry. The more he thought about Tony as a possible suspect, the more he realized it was possible. The man knew Journey well enough to know that her family meant everything.

Coming after me to scare her into dropping the case was a calculated move that backfired.

Not seeing Journey, Laz looked for Dakota and Zenobia. Maybe she had gone with Zen to help her prepare for her performance. Laz shook that thought free. She wouldn't have left without telling him.

Maybe they're in the ladies' room.

He hurried out of the ballroom toward the restrooms, hoping he'd find her there. But that nagging feeling that always warned him when something was wrong stirred inside him.

That motherfucker better not have my wife.

Laz slowed and sent off a quick text to Hamilton.

Can't find Journey. She might be in trouble.

* * *

"Don't do this, Tony," Journey said, struggling to keep up with how fast he was moving. "Anything you've done so far will just be a misdemeanor. But if you take me from this building against my will—a federal employee—the charges increase to a felony and will multiply as a federal offense. Please don't do this. Don't throw your life away like this."

"Just shut up and keep moving."

They were on a lower floor that was too quiet for comfort. They passed another ballroom and a couple of empty meeting rooms. It was clear he didn't have a plan. They were heading in one direction when he stopped suddenly and went the other way.

By now, Laz would be looking for her.

She hoped.

Journey had tried enough kidnapping and rape cases to know she was as good as dead if she left the building. When a side door exit appeared out of nowhere, she knew she had to act fast.

"Wait." She tried to yank her arm free, but he had a death grip on it. "I gotta stop, or I'm going to twist my ankle in these shoes. Then I really won't be able to walk. At least let me take them off."

He slowed. When he glanced down at her feet as if he was considering her request, his grip loosened on her upper arm. It was just enough for her to snatch out of his grasp.

Journey hiked up her dress and took off running in the opposite direction. "Help me!" She screamed at the top of her lungs. "Help!"

Tony grabbed the straps of her dress hanging down her back and yanked her backward with so much force that she crashed to the floor. She landed on her tailbone and cried out as pain surged through her hip and leg.

Tears clouded her eyes, and she feared she'd broken her hip.

Tony tried to get her up, but she started swinging. Journey slammed her small beaded purse against his face, his head, and anywhere else she could hit him. "Help!" she screamed again as she scooted around on the floor, ignoring the sound of ripping material.

She didn't care. She didn't even care that her breasts might be on display since the straps of the halter had loosened.

"Help me!"

Journey tried crawling away, but pain shot up her leg.

"Stop it!" Tony growled and jerked her around to face him. He pointed the gun at her forehead, and her heart stuttered. "You either stop fighting me, or I put a bullet through your head right here and now. Is that what you want?"

If he was going to kill her, he would've done it already, but Journey wasn't taking any chances. Panic pounded through her body like an out-of-control freight train roaring down a steep incline. No doubt that he saw fear on her face—especially if his evil smirk was any indication.

"I thought you'd see it my way," he snarled. "Now get up."

When she struggled to stand, he yanked her up, and she cried out again in pain. He grabbed hold of the two straps holding up her halter dress and roped them around his hand. Journey placed her hand on her chest, trying to breathe as the dress tightened.

"Hey! What's going on down there?" someone called from the other end of the hallway, and Tony cursed.

He jabbed the gun into her side with force, as if reminding her that he could shoot her if she opened her mouth.

This was no longer the gentle man she'd once cared about years ago. She didn't recognize the monster that he had become.

"Move!" he ground out, pushing her toward an open door that led to a stairwell. As she cleared the threshold, Tony jerked her back, and her shoulder connected with the door jamb.

Journey screeched, then collided to the floor with a *thunk*, and when Tony suddenly released her, she scrambled away. It wasn't until she glanced over her shoulder that she understood why he had let her go.

Laz.

Her husband slammed Tony against a wall, knocking the gun from the man's hand, then punched him in the face. They both tumbled to the floor, and Journey started toward them. But Laz pulled out his own gun.

"No! Laz, baby, please don't. Please don't do this!"

Her mind automatically thought in legal terms. If he killed Tony, she could get Laz off with Georgia's *Stand Your Ground* Law. Or maybe self-defense or even defense of another. Her mind whirled, going a hundred miles an hour as she silently freaked out inside.

"Laz...."

Kenton was by her side, pulling her back. He glanced down at her and frowned, then quickly slipped out of his tuxedo jacket to wrap it around her. The state of her dress was the least of Journey's worries. They had to do something.

Journey looked at Laz again, noticing blood on the back of his white dress shirt where the bullet had exited from days ago. Some or all of his stitches must've come loose, and it didn't look like he had a bandage over the wound.

"Kenton, you gotta stop him," she said frantically. Kenton had his arm around her shoulders, holding her in place. "Please stop him. He's already hurt—and I don't want him to kill anyone. Or just let me go to him. I can get him to listen."

"Not while he has a loaded weapon in his hand," Kenton said, more calmly than he should've had in the situation. Then Journey saw Hamilton hurrying toward Laz.

Thank God. If anyone could talk some sense into him, it was Ham.

"Laz, man. What the hell?" Hamilton said, slowly approaching him. "If you going to shoot him, do it. Or put the damn gun down."

"He put his fucking hands on my wife!" Laz said, and Journey flinched at the torture she heard in his voice. Her heart broke for her husband. "His ass ain't walking out of here alive."

"Come on, dude. Don't do this."

"My child could've been killed the other day!" Laz roared.

"But she wasn't, and in a couple of days, you'll be holding your baby in your arms. But if you shoot this piece of shit, there's no telling how long you'll sit in county lockup. He's not worth it, man."

"He ordered a hit on me. I could've been killed, and what about Nazir? He didn't deserve what he got! This asshole didn't give a damn about any of us." Laz cocked his gun. "Nah, he's gotta die. Then we'll be even."

Journey gasped. "Laz, please."

"Just shoot me," Tony said. "I have nothing left. I don't care."

"If you insist."

"Don't!" Hamilton yelled, the word crackling through the air like roaring thunder. "Don't do this. Put the gun down. Now!" he roared.

"I can't let him get away with this," Laz whispered.

She closed her eyes, unable to watch anymore. If he was going to kill Tony, she didn't want to witness it, but she couldn't walk away either. Her husband needed her, and she felt so helpless.

"Laz, Journey is right here," Hamilton said, and she eased her eyes open. "You don't want her to see you shoot this piece of shit. She'll never be able to unsee that. Give me the gun—or set it down on the floor."

Laz grabbed the front of Tony's shirt, lifting him slightly, then slammed Tony's head against the floor with such force Journey felt the pain through her own body.

The cops had shown up with their guns drawn and eased closer.

"Please don't hurt him. He was just protecting me," she said in a rush and started toward them, but Kenton stopped her with a hand on her shoulders.

"Jay," he said in warning. "He'll be okay. They won't move in as long as Hamilton can get Laz to lower his weapon."

Hamilton was former police and still knew so many cops and detectives on the force. Surprisingly, they let him handle Laz. Journey just prayed that their friend could get through to him.

Especially since he wasn't listening to her.

Laz switched the gun to his left hand, and Journey thought he was getting ready to set it on the floor. But then he slammed his right fist into Tony's face so hard that he knocked the man unconscious. At least Journey hoped that was the case.

Laz lowered the weapon and set it on the floor. He lifted his right hand in the air. But the way he grimaced as he struggled to raise his left hand, it was clear he was in pain. Tons of cops moved in at once, and so did Kenton.

Before Journey could take two steps, Remy was in her face.

"ADA Dimas, I'm glad you're okay. Come with me so we can talk," he said, his voice kind as he tried to lead her away with a loose hold on her elbow.

"I'm not going anywhere without my husband," she snapped, especially nowhere with him after the way he had treated Laz in the hospital. The thought of that day only made her angrier, and she snatched her arm out of his hold.

Remy sighed, then growled under his breath. "I need to get a statement from—"

"What part of 'I'm not going anywhere without my husband' don't you understand, detective? Now move out of my way! Now!" she screamed, adrenaline pulsing through her veins.

"Journey!" Laz yelled. "Where is she?"

"I'm here," she called out and tried to move around Remy, but he blocked her path. It took every bit of control in her not to knee him in the balls. "You either put cuffs on me or get the hell out of my way," she seethed. She wasn't a violent person, but she suddenly wanted to plow her fist into his face.

"Is there a problem here?" Kenton asked and eased his big body between her and Remy, towering over both of them. "She won't leave without answering whatever questions you have, but right now, considering what she just went through, let her at least talk to her husband."

"Stand down, Remy," Ted said upon his approach. Journey pushed her way through the small crowd until she reached Laz. The cops were about to cuff him.

"No!" she bellowed. "Absolutely not! If you even think about cuffing him, I'll have the police commissioner down here so fast that your heads will spin. My husband was protecting me. He is not the aggressor! Now back the hell up!"

Laz pulled her into his arms, and tears stung Journey's eyes. He held her so tight that she was sure he would crush her lungs. She could barely breathe.

"I thought I lost you," Laz choked out, tears in his voice.

"I'm right here, and I'm okay," she said in a rush, unable to keep her tears at bay.

She tried to pull out of his vise-grip hold, but he wouldn't let go. She stopped trying when she heard him sniff.

"I love you so much," she said, kissing the side of his neck since he was still holding her tightly. "Thank you for saving me."

"Always, baby," he said hoarsely. "Always."

Chapter Twenty-Six

"You really should be having this done at the hospital," Doctor Mateo Gonzalez—Angelo's brother—grumbled.

Mateo was the only doctor Laz knew personally, and he reluctantly came to the hotel to stitch him back up. Some of Laz's sutures had come undone, and since his gunshot wound hadn't completely healed, he'd had to get them redone. His shoulder and arm throbbed like a bitch, but at least the numbing cream that Mateo had used helped with the pain.

"The entrance wound is fine. No sutures are needed. Unfortunately, the exit wound is open; but doesn't appear to be infected. If you notice any discharge, swelling, or if it looks or feels like something is wrong, don't call me. Get to the hospital immediately."

"It'll be fine," Laz said absently, ignoring Mateo's grumbling about how he never listens.

Laz's attention was on Journey, asleep on the king-size bed. She hadn't said much in the last hour, and he was worried about her. Wanting to keep an eye on her and touch her, he had moved his chair from the dining area to the bedroom, needing to be close. Holding her hand, he gently rubbed his thumb over her soft skin.

"Are you sure she's all right?"

Before the doctor started stitching him up, Laz had demanded he check Journey first. Besides a massive bruise on her hip and a few on her arms, she was okay.

"Yeah, she's going to be all right, and it's not unusual to crash after an adrenaline rush."

One minute she seemed okay, and then on the way to their hotel room, she was light-headed and exhausted.

"I told you I was fine," Journey said sleepily without opening her eyes.

Laz smiled when she squeezed his hand.

He released a pent-up breath that he'd been holding for what seemed like hours.

He couldn't stop thinking about how the situation could've turned out differently, especially after learning that Tony had been the one to kill Journey's witness, Fred. Laz didn't know the man had that type of gangster behavior in him. Tony always came across like a choirboy, doing the right thing and not causing trouble.

Now more than ever, Laz was glad he'd gotten to Journey before anything else happened to her. He'd had more scares this past week than he'd had his entire life. When he couldn't find her, Hamilton and Kenton had joined in on the search. They all feared Tony had taken her from the building, and Laz was prepared to do anything to find her.

He had searched the bathrooms and the other spaces that *Save Our Boys* had rented out. It wasn't until he went down one level that he heard Journey screaming. From there, he'd been on autopilot. The moment he reached the hallway, he saw the back of Tony's body, and it was as if someone had waved a red scarf in front of him. Laz charged.

Had Hamilton and Kenton not shown up when they had, he was sure he would've killed the bastard. Hell, he still might. All Laz had to do was make a call. Whether Tony was walking down the street or behind bars, there were people who could get to him anywhere and end his worthless life.

I can't make the call.

If Tony ended up dead in the near future, Journey would assume he had something to do with it. Nope, he wouldn't stoop to Tony's level and order a hit. He didn't have to. The man wasn't made for prison, and it gave Laz pleasure knowing that he'd probably get his ass kicked more than a few times while locked up.

"Sit still," Mateo demanded, and Laz flinched when he felt a pinch at the back of his shoulder. "Almost done."

"This has been a long-ass night," Laz said to no one in particular.

Instead of taking him and Journey down to the police station for questioning, Ted agreed to do it in their hotel suite. Per protocol, they'd been separated, with Laz being questioned in the bedroom and Journey in the living room area.

Laz had thought it odd when Kenton had insisted that Ted get someone other than Remy to question Journey. It wasn't until after the cops left that Kenton filled him in on the altercation between Jay and the asshole Remy. All the more reason why Laz hated the detective. Hopefully, he wouldn't have any more dealings with the man.

"All right, I'm done," Mateo said. He scooted his chair back and stood over Laz, inspecting the stitching one last time. "I think you're good to go, but can you please try to refrain from fighting? That wound will never close up if you keep pulling the sutures loose."

"Fine. No more fighting," Laz said quietly as he eased his hand out of Journey's grasp. She had finally fallen asleep, and he didn't want to wake her.

Mateo gathered his equipment, and he and Laz moved to the living room. Laz was surprised to see that Hamilton and Dakota were still there. While Hamilton was murmuring on his cell phone, Dakota was dozing on the sofa.

"On a serious note," Mateo said when he was ready to leave, "I'm glad you guys are all right."

"Thanks, man. Me too. It's been a rough few days. I appreciate you doing a house call."

"No problem. You know I'm always here for you and the guys, but I'm thinking about getting Mase to put me on retainer. "

Laz snorted. "Our own resident doctor. Sounds good to me."

They said their goodbyes, and Laz locked up behind him. He leaned against the door and released a sigh of relief as he glanced around the open space. The suite was a nice size and decorated in browns and blues. It looked like a small apartment with a living room, dining room combo, a tiny kitchen area, and a second bathroom off the living room. The space was perfect for a little R&R.

Laz strolled past the kitchen and returned to the living room just as Hamilton disconnected his call.

"Got some good news," Hamilton said.

"Great. I can use some." Suddenly feeling the effects of the evening, Laz rubbed his forehead and eased into one of the cushioned chairs in the dining area.

"They found Tamar Warner."

Laz perked up, glad he'd be able to give Journey the good news when she woke up. "Where'd they find her?"

"Savannah, Georgia. She was staying with a cousin, but

when that same cousin found out there was a reward for any information on Tamar, she called the hotline."

Laz grunted and yawned. "That's messed up, but good for us."

"Yeah, based on my source, the Feds picked Tamar up an hour ago. She'll be formally arraigned in Federal court on Monday."

Good. At least Journey wouldn't have to deal with her old nemesis as she finished pulling her case against Dennis Stratton together.

There was a knock on the door, and Laz flinched. His hand automatically went to the back of his waistband for his weapon, only to remember that the cops had it.

Damn.

"Relax, man," Hamilton said as he walked past him. "I'll get it. The front desk called and said you had a delivery earlier this evening. I had them send it up. That's probably who's at the door."

When Hamilton returned, Laz accepted the black bag from him and glanced inside, knowing immediately what it was.

"Thanks. Actually, thanks for everything you did tonight. Sorry about what happened downstairs." Laz appreciated his friend trying to talk him off the ledge with Tony, even if he struggled to listen.

"No apology necessary. I would've behaved just like you, and I know you would've been there to talk me down."

"Umm, I'm not too sure about that," Laz chuckled, and Hamilton joined in. "I probably would've been the one encouraging you to take the bastard out."

"Good point. That's why we need the Ashtons and the Kentons in our life. But seriously, I'm proud of you. The old Laz might've smoked him before thinking about the consequences."

His friend was right. He was an eye-for-an-eye kind of guy. If someone did him wrong, he'd come for them and make them regret ever knowing him. He might not have used the best judgment with the shooters, but he was glad Hamilton had been able to stop him from killing Tony.

Progress. I'm making progress.

* * *

The next morning, Journey didn't physically feel like her usual self, but mentally, she was happy to be alive. Her emotional state was a different story. It would take time to get past the fact that she could've been killed last night. But knowing that her family was safe would go a long way.

She was so glad that she and Laz had had the foresight to book the hotel suite the night before. This morning, they'd had breakfast and were now lounging in bed watching television.

"I'm glad they found her," she said of Tamar. There was a breaking news report on the TV screen showing the arrest from the night before. "People like her make it hard to trust political figures."

"Yeah," Laz agreed as he sipped a cup of coffee. "Do you think you'll reach out to her or go see her?" Laz asked.

"No. She's not a friend, and she's no longer a part of my case against Dennis Stratton. She belongs to the Feds now. She and I have nothing to discuss."

After talking to Prentice earlier, Journey had learned that Tony had no knowledge of Tamar accepting bribes. He thought they were really building a relationship until she vanished, going on the run after news broke about her accepting bribes. Tamar, on the other hand, knew Tony was up to something but claimed she didn't know what, according to her statement to the police.

For some reason, Journey believed Tony, even though he'd held her at gunpoint. He really seemed to care for Tamar, whereas it sounded like the feeling wasn't mutual.

"All right, enough of this. I don't want to hear the name Tamar or Tony anytime soon," Laz said and turned off the television. "I have something for you."

Laz eased off the bed. She was glad to see him wearing his sling again and hoped this time he'd allow his shoulder wound to heal. He left the bedroom and returned seconds later with a bag and handed it to her.

Journey glanced inside. "A gift? What's the occasion?" she asked and pulled out the square black velvet box.

He reclaimed his position on the bed. "Just open it."

She lifted the lid and sucked in a breath. Inside was the most beautiful platinum heart-shaped locket she'd ever seen. It was hanging from a silver chain, and there were words in script lettering across the front.

She swallowed hard as she read the inscription. *You're always in our hearts.*

"Oh, Laz," she whispered, getting choked up at the sentiment.

He pulled her against him and kissed the side of her head. "Open the locket."

She did, and inside the charm was a photo of him on the left. Journey smiled, surprised that he had used a picture of himself smiling when he was always trying to look intimidating. On the right side was a picture of her daughter's precious face.

"Ohhh..." she said with her hand on her chest and then looked up at Laz. "Thank you, baby. This is so beautiful and extremely thoughtful."

He carefully pulled the jewelry from the box. When he tried to unclasp it, Journey took over, then fastened the necklace around her neck.

"I need you to wear it at all times," he said, and she nodded. "The diamond at the top of the heart conceals a GPS chip, and it works even if you're deep in a cave. I never want to experience not being able to find you again." Journey started to speak, but he spoke over her. "And I promise, just like with the watch, I'll only have you tracked if there is an emergency."

"I know, and I'm not worried about that. What I was going to say is, I want my watch back. It was so much more than a tracker. It was one of the first gifts you ever gave me. It's sentimental."

Laz studied her for a few minutes before saying, "Is that why Kenton had to put you in a headlock to get it off your wrist?"

Journey's mouth dropped open. "What? Is that what he told you?"

Laz flashed a crooked grin, then laughed. "Nah, I'm just messing with you."

She swatted his good arm.

"But I did hear that you didn't want to give it up."

"The watch means everything to me, but I also thought he was taking it because you no longer wanted me protected."

Laz reached into the drawer of the nightstand and pulled out the watch. "I had a feeling that's what you thought, but Jay, I'll never stop protecting you. My life is nothing without you. Don't you know that? Yeah, we had our problems, and I know I said some things, but that was just me being an ass. I love you, baby. Don't ever doubt that. I'm a hundred percent committed to you and the life that we've built."

Journey swallowed, trying not to get emotional. Whenever she thought she couldn't love him anymore, he said or did something that contradicted that.

"Have I mentioned how much I love you?" she asked, her heart overflowing with love.

"Umm, yeah. I think you have mentioned it a few times, but maybe you can show me."

A smile spread across her face, and she pushed him back against the pillows. "I think I can handle that."

Journey covered his mouth with hers and kissed him, knowing without a doubt they were going to spend the rest of their lives loving each other.

Epilogue

Three months later....

"Oh, my goodness, Gen. She's beautiful," Journey gushed as she held her precious niece. "Hey, Zuri Noelle. I'm your Auntie Jay. I'm so glad you're here."

"Not as glad as I am," Geneva mumbled and scooted down in the bed. "Why didn't you tell me how much it would hurt? I almost lost my shit, *literally*, and the pain...Oh. My. God. *Never* again. No wonder you stopped at one kid."

Journey sputtered a laugh. "You read like fifty books on childbirth. Surely, one of the authors mentioned that it was going to hurt. Besides, I couldn't tell you because I forgot. Once you hold all of this cuteness in your arms, you kinda forget about—"

"Something is wrong with your ass if you can forget what I just went through for ten hours. *Ten frickin' hours*, Jay!" She rubbed her forehead, exhaustion evident. "Never again. I shouldn't have let Myles's *fine ass* talk me into having sex with him."

"Girl, you need to quit. Anyone who knows both of you knows that you were probably the aggressor. Also, you're going to have to clean up your language. Otherwise, this little one's first words will be curse words. Actually, you and Laz both, because he's been reverting back to his old ways of every other word being a curse word.

Geneva grumbled something, but Journey couldn't stop looking at the sleeping baby in her arms. She couldn't help wondering what it would be like to have another child. Her window of opportunity was closing quickly, but there was still a little time. She already knew Laz wanted to try for a boy, but up until a few months ago, there was no way Journey could envision bringing another child into their world.

Now? Maybe.

It was official.

Yesterday was her last day in the DA's office.

She still couldn't believe that she'd been brave enough to walk away from a job she thought she couldn't live without. The days of long hours, stressful cases, and thoughts of being the next DA were gone. She thought it would be hard to leave. Instead, it felt as if an enormous weight had lifted from her shoulders as she closed some pending cases.

The one that gave her pause was the Stratton case. At first, she considered staying until after the trial and the case was closed but instead decided to hand it off to another prosecutor. She'd had enough and knew it was time to move on.

Journey had no regrets. If the last few months had taught her anything, it was that there was nothing more important than family.

When Zuri started to fuss, Journey gave her to Geneva, who immediately started feeding her.

"She really is beautiful, isn't she?" Geneva said with awe as she fingered the baby's headful of black curls.

"Yes, she is." Journey sat in a nearby chair. "Are you ready for all of this?"

"No. Not at all. You're always talking about how hard it is juggling motherhood, being a wife, and having a career. I don't know how I'm going to do it."

"You're going to do it just like the rest of us. One day at a time, and don't be like me. Don't ever forget what's most important."

Geneva's eyebrows dipped. "Which is?"

"Family. Gen, don't ever take Myles and Zuri for granted. When Laz was shot...." Journey shook off the shiver that went through her. "It scared me to death how close I came to losing him and Ari. Life is so short and unpredictable. Don't put work before those you love. I learned that the hard way. Yes, there will be times when you might have to, but don't make a habit of it. They are too precious to come second to anything," Journey said as she rubbed the back of the baby's hand.

"Dude, you do realize I played a major part in all of this, right?" Myles was saying when he and Laz entered the room. "Not only that, Zuri looks just like me."

"Did you not hear me say she's gorgeous? Except for your mocha skin tone, she looks nothing like you," Laz insisted. "What you need to be doing is thinking about how you're going to keep these little peanut-headed boys away from her. You're a girl dad now. That comes with a lot of responsibility."

Journey and Geneva shook their heads as the guys went back and forth, talking nonsense.

"How did it go FaceTiming with Collin?" Journey asked Geneva.

"It went well. The book you guys bought him about being a big brother helped. He's anxious to see Zuri, and he's already planning on taking her to Disney World with him and Arielle next time."

Journey smiled at that. Arielle talked about their trip for a month after they returned. To say she and Collin had fun was an understatement. Journey would be forever grateful to her parents. The trip had been timely. She and Laz didn't have to worry about their daughter while dealing with the situation with Tony. They were also able to work on their marriage and were closer than they'd ever been, and Journey was beside herself with happiness.

"Okay, we better get going so you guys can bond with your little one, and I'm sure Mom is anxious to get back here to her new grandbaby."

Their mom and Myles had been in the delivery room with Geneva while Journey and Laz looked after Collin. Arielle had been thrilled to have her cousin spend the night, and Journey had been delighted to get a break. When her parents left the hospital, they took Journey and Laz's place with the kids.

After saying their goodbyes, Journey and Laz walked hand in hand to the parking garage. When they reached his new Chevy Tahoe, he backed her against the vehicle and kissed her.

Journey slipped her arms around Laz's neck, glad she no longer had to worry about his wound. It had finally healed. He had a small scar on the front of his shoulder and a larger one on the back of it, but no mobility problems, thank goodness. He was lucky to be alive, and Journey would never take him or his love for granted.

When the kiss ended, Laz lifted his head but didn't release her. "Now that you're unemployed, what do you think about us having another baby?" he asked, wiggling his eyebrows.

"Funny you should ask."

Laz's smile dropped, and his hands fell from her hips. "Wait. You're preg—"

"Nooo!" she said quickly and looped her arms around him. "I'm sorry, I didn't mean to imply that I was. What I meant was the thought had crossed my mind while I was holding Zuri. If we...." Her cell phone rang, and she dug it from the side pocket of her handbag.

"Hello?"

"Journey?"

Her brows furrowed at the unfamiliar voice. "Yes. Who's calling?"

"This is Nina from Randolph and Tate."

Journey's heart leaped into her chest, and she grinned at Laz, who was looking at her questioningly. "Hey, Nina. How are you?"

"I'm great. I'm calling because I'd like to officially offer you the job. We would love to have you join our team."

Journey did a little shimmy as she listened to the woman explain the offer that paid more than she'd been making at the DA's office. The benefits were similar, but what appealed to Journey most were the hours—only forty hours a week max—and she'd be working with nonprofit agencies.

"Nina, thank you for the offer. It all sounds wonderful, but can I get back to you tomorrow? I want to discuss it with my husband."

"Of course. I look forward to hearing from you soon."

"Sounds good, and thanks again!" Journey said, barely able to contain her excitement before disconnecting the call. She held the phone to her chest, grinning from ear to ear, knowing that this was the start of a new chapter in her life. The type of work she'd be doing was exactly what she wanted to do.

"Okay, what's going on?" Laz asked, smiling. He knew she

had interviewed with two law firms that only worked with nonprofit organizations.

"I'm no longer unemployed!" she squealed. "The Randolph and Tate Firm offered me the position."

"Oh, wow. Congratulations, baby!" He pulled her into his arms and kissed her. "We're going to have to celebrate."

Journey told him about the position. The idea of doing what she loved while keeping her promise to Laz about not working crazy hours only made her more excited.

"That's amazing. It sounds like a perfect fit. I'm proud of you."

"Thank you."

"Wait. Hold up" Laz held her at arm's length. "Does this mean having another baby is off the table?"

Journey tapped her finger against her chin. "Hmm...well, I guess everything's negotiable. How about we go home, and you can...plead your case."

With a cocky grin spreading across his handsome face, Laz slipped his arm around her and pulled her against his hard body.

"There you go lawyering me again, but I'm here for it. Let me take you home so I can present you with my opening statement."

Journey laughed. "Bring it!"

Next Book In Series

Thank you for reading COMMITTED! Laz and Journey are one of my favorite couples, and I hope you enjoyed revisiting with them. Stay tuned for the next book in the Atlanta's Finest series - Parker's story!

Want more romantic suspense? Check out the Reunited Series starting with **BLUE ROSES.**

And don't miss out on the Jenkins & Sons Construction series starting with **LOVE UNDER CONTRACT!**

If you enjoyed this book, consider leaving a review on retailer's sites, review sites or social media outlets.

Join Sharon's Mailing List

To get sneak peeks of upcoming stories and to hear about giveaways that Sharon is sponsoring, click **here** to join her mailing list.

Other Titles By Sharon

Atlanta's Finest Series

Atlanta's Finest Series

A Passionate Kiss (book 1 - prequel)

Vindicated (book 2)

Indebted (book 3)

Accused (book 4)

Betrayed (book 5)

Hunted (book 6)

Tempted (book 7)

Committed (book 8)

Jenkins & Sons Construction Series (Contemporary Romance)

Love Under Contract (book 1)

Proposal for Love (book 2)

A Lesson on Love (book 3)

Unplanned Love (book 4)

Jenkins Family Series (Contemporary Romance)

Best Woman for the Job (Short Story Prequel)
Still the Best Woman for the Job (book 1)
All You'll Ever Need (book 2)
Tempting the Artist (book 3)
Negotiating for Love (book 4)
Seducing the Boss Lady (book 5)
Love at Last (Holiday Novella)
When Love Calls (Novella)
More Than Love (Novella)

Reunited Series (Romantic Suspense)
Blue Roses (book 1)
Secret Rendezvous (Prequel to Rendezvous with Danger)
Rendezvous with Danger (book 2)
Truth or Consequences (book 3)
Operation Midnight (book 4)
Casino Heat (book 5)

Stand Alones
Something New ("Edgy" Sweet Romance)
Legal Seduction (Harlequin Kimani – Contemporary Romance)
Sin City Temptation (Harlequin Kimani – Contemporary Romance)
A Dose of Passion (Harlequin Kimani – Contemporary Romance)
Model Attraction (Harlequin Kimani – Contemporary Romance)
Soul's Desire (Unparalleled Love series)
Show Me (Irresistible Husband series)
His to Protect (Harlequin Romantic Suspense)
His to Defend (Harlequin Romantic Suspense)
Business Not As Usual (Romantic Comedy)

About the Author

USA Today bestselling author Sharon C. Cooper loves anything involving romance with a happily-ever-after, whether in books, movies, or real life. She writes contemporary romance, as well as romantic suspense and enjoys rainy days, carpet picnics, and peanut butter and jelly sandwiches. Her stories have won numerous awards over the years, and when Sharon isn't writing, she's hanging out with her amazing husband, doing volunteer work, or reading a good book (a romance of course). To read more about Sharon and her novels, visit www.sharoncooper.net

Made in the USA
Middletown, DE
08 July 2022